"I can fulfill your wildest fantasies," Nate murmured

Annie shivered as his warm breath laved her ear. She leaned back into his body as they stood together on the rooftop garden. She felt his growing hardness against her.

"Just tell me what you want." He squeezed her breasts gently and she thought she might faint. But he held her fast while his hands worked themselves down to her waist. He started to untie her dress, and she hesitated.

Did Nate intend to remove her dress here, in public? *Make love to her, in public?*

"No one will see. It's dark," he urged with a smile in his voice.

He tugged at the dress and it opened. The cool spring air nipped at her exposed nipples. Annie hadn't been able to resist. She'd worn the sexy tiger-print lingerie he'd requested. The thin silk covered very little.

She should tell him to stop. But her body felt wet and slick and hot. And after all, he was about to fulfill *one* of her wildest fantasies....

Dear Reader,

Writing for Blaze is a bit of a departure for me. Normally I write romantic suspense for the Intrigue line, but when I heard about Blaze, I thought I could write something a little different—erotic thrillers.

I wanted to use an urban setting, something I knew a lot about since I'm a native Chicagoan. I picked an up-and-coming neighborhood and then I populated it with characters that I hope you'll grow to love as much as I do. Annie, Nick and Helen have been best friends since college. They even quit their jobs to strike out on their own and start their own businesses. And they'll support each other as they fall in love and meet danger head-on.

Annie's story was a *Sheer Pleasure* to write. I hope you'll agree and watch for *Improper Conduct,* coming next in my CHICAGO HEAT miniseries.

I love to hear from readers! You can contact me at:
P.O. Box 578297, Chicago, IL 60657-8297 or e-mail
Patricia@PatriciaRosemoor.com. Check out my Web site at
www.PatriciaRosemoor.com

Happy reading,

Patricia Rosemoor

Books by Patricia Rosemoor

HARLEQUIN INTRIGUE

563—THE LONE WOLF'S CHILD
567—A RANCHER'S VOW
629—SOMEONE TO PROTECT HER

SHEER PLEASURE

Patricia Rosemoor

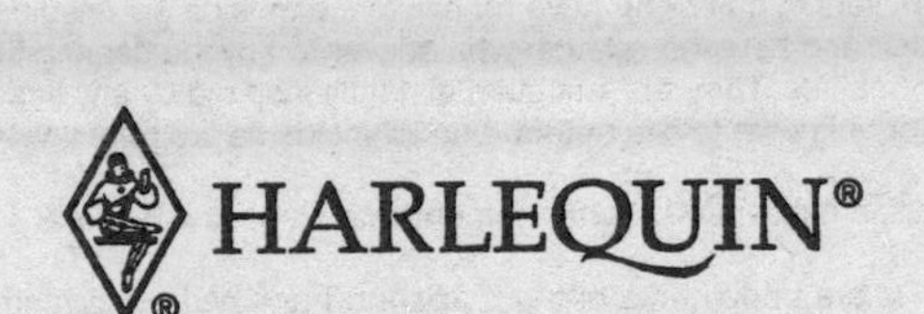

TORONTO • NEW YORK • LONDON
AMSTERDAM • PARIS • SYDNEY • HAMBURG
STOCKHOLM • ATHENS • TOKYO • MILAN • MADRID
PRAGUE • WARSAW • BUDAPEST • AUCKLAND

To my husband, Edward, in appreciation for
your continuing support of anything I choose to do.

And to my editor, Birgit Davis-Todd,
who took a chance on something a little different.

ISBN 0-373-79039-2

SHEER PLEASURE

This edition published by arrangement with Harlequin Books S.A.

Visit us at www.eHarlequin.com

Printed in U.S.A.

1

Dear Annie,

While others may wonder about the success of your lingerie shop, I wonder about you—about the woman hidden in the brown paper wrapper.

If I peeled away the layers, would I find a woman in filmy, lacy, see-through garments? A woman who longed for me to trust that she is more than she appears to be?

What are your secret fantasies, I wonder?

And would you give me the chance to find out for myself?

An Admirer

HER HAND TREMBLING, Annie Wilder set down on her desk the ecru stationery with the lacy texture across the top. Romantic stationery for a man to use, she thought. It kind of went with that comment about lacy, see-through garments.

She should be scared. So why wasn't she?

Some man whom she might or might not know had sent her this anonymous letter and her imagination was sparked. She was curious about the sender. A little turned on. Definitely not afraid.

That scared her more than the letter itself.

She should have her head examined.

To distract herself, Annie ventured back out to the shop, a deep-rose cave whose corners were draped with gold-shot cream swaths cascading from rings on the ceiling. Midnight-blue and vanilla-cream satin sheets filled the shelves on one short wall, bottles and pots of potions and creams the other. Passing the rack of teddies, Annie let her hand brush the jewel-tone bits of silk and satin and lace as she made her way back to the display she'd been setting up before she'd decided to check the day's mail.

She was alone this evening—Gloria Delgado, her assistant manager and only full-time employee, had gone home early—but she felt safe enough with the front door locked.

Outside the plate-glass windows, dusk had fallen over the street and traffic had intensified. Diners and dancers and denizens of the neighborhood whirled from cars, buses and the nearby elevated rapid transit station, to swirl down the street along with occasional debris picked up by errant warm breezes. People looking for an evening's pleasure would surely find it in the restaurants, cafés and clubs lining North, Damen and Milwaukee, the commercial avenues of Bucktown and Wicker Park, two abutting Chicago north-side neighborhoods that met at this six-corner crossroads.

Concentrating on her undertaking, Annie arranged two dozen packets of condoms according to color and turned the simple display into a sensual rainbow.

Then she stepped back and snickered at her fanciful handiwork.

Who in the world, looking at a small woman wearing a long black pullover and leggings, her brown hair braided, her face sans embellishment but for a pair of frameless glasses, would ever imagine that she was capable of sexual whimsy?

"An Admirer" would. She thought again of the anonymous missive in her office.

At least one man had obviously looked beneath the surface to find the real owner of Annie's Attic, lingerie playground—and the most talked about, written about and picketed business in the neighborhood.

The lingerie itself didn't have people buzzing, but the way she displayed her wares to inspire fantasies did. After all, wasn't that the point of wearing expensive pieces of fragile fabric that would rip at a rough touch?

For a moment the thought caught her, an image rolling through her head like a movie.

She strolled along the beach in see-through undies, the envy of the women lounging around her, the object of lust of the men. The cast of thousands faded out, leaving only one man, faceless, but with thick dark hair and a body like Adonis. He moved behind her, cupped her breasts, and with his thumbs only, tugged lightly at the straps of her bra. The fabric shredded instantly, freeing her flesh.

She arched back....

A banging at the front window startled her and pulled her back into the moment. Heart thudding, Annie whipped around to see Nathaniel Bishop, owner of Cornerstone Realty and this building, on the other side of the plate glass.

A little breathless, she rushed to the door and unlocked it.

His eyebrows arched when he got a good look at her face. "I didn't mean to scare you."

"Startle," Annie countered, covering for herself as she stood back to let him in. Surely he couldn't tell what she'd been thinking. Warmth surged through her, anyway. "You just startled me, that's all."

"I stand corrected."

He stood more than six feet tall, the dark business suit making him appear sleek and successful...and, to Annie's mind, just a little too boring. Too bad. He was certainly a looker, with blue-black hair and piercing blue eyes, a slight cleft in his strong chin. But that chin topped a conservative white shirt and a conservative navy-and-red tie that reflected the man himself. Not the kind of guy a girl had fantasies over.

Annie suddenly realized he was staring at her display of condoms.

"New product line?"

A reasonable question, considering she sold mood music, games for lovers and a line of exotic oils in addition to the lingerie.

Heat crept up her neck. "Not exactly. I just thought I would display them more..."

"Provocatively?"

His tone stirred the short hairs at the back of her neck. "I was going to say prominently."

"You certainly did that."

He turned his gaze to her and she caught her breath. That look in his eyes... For a moment she thought she saw something she'd missed before.

She definitely felt as if she'd been caught with her hand in the cookie jar. Make that condom jar.

"I just thought I would promote customers taking

some responsibility. I was even thinking of giving away a couple of freebies with every sale, what with the fantasies I've been told my lingerie inspires."

"You wear lingerie that inspires fantasies?"

Now he sounded amused, causing heat to flood her cheeks. Great.

"You know what I meant. The lingerie I *sell* inspires fantasies."

"Then you don't wear your own product?"

"Well, yes...I mean..."

She was caught.

And Nathaniel's amusement had subtly changed. He was still smiling, but somehow his lips seemed softer...more sensual. She could imagine them covering hers, trailing a damp kiss down her throat, nuzzling her breasts through her serviceable black cotton pullover.

Startled when her nipples hardened, Annie crossed her arms in front of her chest in case it showed through the layers of gauzy underwear and black cotton. Nathaniel Bishop was far from the type of man who would make her hormones race. That letter had sparked her fantasies, and he had just happened to be around was all.

"It's getting late," she said, straightening a rack of black and red leather waist cinchers that didn't need straightening. "I need to head for home soon."

"Someone keeping dinner for you?"

Annie grinned. "If only Rock could learn to cook."

"Rock. New boyfriend?"

"New cat. I found him in the alley last week. He was scruffy and starving. His little sides were practically sticking together. I'm working on that, though."

Nathanial's features softened. "Why did you name him Rock?"

"Because he was trying to eat one."

"Poor guy, but lucky him to find you," he said. "I won't hold you up, then. I just stopped by to make sure you weren't having any more problems with the faucet."

"You did a fine job of replacing the washer the other day," she assured him.

Nathaniel Bishop was a dream landlord. No sooner did she call him with a concern than he was immediately on the problem, no matter how small. A man in a designer suit willing to change a washer for a tenant was pretty damn impressive. No wonder he appeared so successful, even though he couldn't be much past thirty.

"No other complaints?" he asked.

"Not a one."

"If there's anything you need—and I do mean *anything*—just call me."

"I'll do that."

"Good. I'll be going, then."

He hesitated as if he meant to say more. But if so, he changed his mind, for he nodded and headed toward the door. As he did, Annie glimpsed through the window the broad back of a man rapidly moving away from the store. She thought she recognized Vincent Zavadinski, the man running for reelection as alderman, who was quite vocal in his disapproval of her business.

"Remember, anything," Nathaniel repeated, bringing her focus back to him.

"Got it," she assured him. "See you."

Annie was sure that she *would* see Nathaniel Bishop, and when she least expected it. He had an office in the building and stopped by every few days to see how things were going. She suspected he wanted to make certain there was no damage to his property. Annie's Attic did have its detractors, some of whom had picketed her business more than once since it had opened three months before. Just last week, someone had thrown eggs against her windows, she supposed in an attempt to hide her display.

No doubt Nathaniel was keeping a close watch on his investment.

HE WATCHED THE LIGHTS in Annie's Attic go out, one at a time, leaving only those illuminating the display window.

There, a male mannequin, sprawled on cushions, wearing only a pair of black silk boxers covered with dozens of bright red lips, and a pair of matching socks. His female counterpart sat upright, posed as if removing a sweater, revealing a red satin bra beneath. The window had changed over the course of the week. The couple had started out fully dressed, but one article of clothing at a time had been stripped from them—a clever idea that had brought potential customers back again and again to see what came next. Between the pair of mannequins sat a board game called Deep Undercover, what looked to be a lovers' version of strip poker.

He'd like to go undercover with Annie Wilder. The thought had obsessed him since she'd set up shop.

The front door opened and she stepped outside to lock it. He moved deeper into the shadows so she wouldn't see him watching.

He knew everything about her—the hours she kept, where she lived, where she played.

It was only a matter of time.

DECIDING THAT SHE COULD use a strong cup of coffee to energize her on the way home, Annie rounded the corner and ducked into Helen's Cybercafé, located on one of the six corners and adjacent to Annie's Attic. The place was trendy but comfortable, with crackled pale yellow walls, an overstuffed couch and two upholstered chairs near a fireplace, several wooden tables and chairs for either two or four and, along one wall, a bank of computers.

Best of all, though, her friend, owner Helen Rhodes, was working behind the counter at the cappuccino machine.

"Hey!" Annie called out.

"Annie, hey," Nick Novak replied from directly behind her.

Giving her a start. Where had he materialized from to follow her so closely into the café?

She noticed he was carrying the equipment bag that held his videocam—so he must have been out on a shoot.

"It's dinnertime and my stomach is ready to protest." Nick patted the abs he worked so hard to perfect. "Let's order a pizza."

"Uh, excuse me, Mr. Smart Aleck Novak," Helen said, "but I do serve food here."

Moseying over to the bank of computers, Nick sat at the only available station, shoved his equipment bag under the table and turned his back on her. "But I want *good* food."

He attacked the keys as Helen glared at the back of his neck. But staying mad at Nick was useless, as they both knew—he let anger roll off of him like rainwater—and Helen quickly turned her attention to Annie.

"Your usual?"

"Please. To go."

"What's the hurry?" Nick asked.

"Rock."

"That scraggly little beast can wait a while longer." Nick left the computer, which was downloading e-mail, to join her. "I haven't seen you in a couple of days. Sit. Spill."

Annie sat at the closest table for four. "Spill what?"

He peered closely at her, his golden wolf eyes narrowing. Nick had an intuitive side...and a dark side, as well, she knew.

"You have a certain glow about you," he said. "A new man?"

"Not exactly."

He changed his inflection. "You haven't gone over to the other side?"

She glared at Nick. "Who would you torture if you didn't have me?"

"Helen."

"He does it out of frustration because he can't get a date," Helen said.

"I have plenty of dates."

"You mean one-night stands, don't you?" Helen asked. "Once with you is enough for any woman."

Unsuccessfully trying to appear wounded, Nick asked, "How did this conversation become about me?"

"You asked for it," Annie said, grinning at him.

Helen arrived at the table with the coffee to go. "He's right. You are glowing."

Warmth climbed up Annie's neck into her cheeks. "It's nothing. Just a letter."

"What kind of letter?"

"A fan letter...I—I guess."

The real reason she'd stopped by the café.

Annie pulled the envelope out of her pocket and handed it to Nick. Still standing, Helen leaned over his shoulder and looked on as he unfolded the missive and read it.

A shiver went through Annie as she listened to the seductive words being read aloud in a deep male voice, but it was a good shiver.

"Hmm, a creative meet and greet," Nick said.

Helen countered, "Spooky, if you ask me."

Which was what Annie had been afraid of. Crestfallen, she asked, "You really think so?"

"He didn't sign his name, did he?" Helen reminded her. "Maybe it's that weirdo who keeps insisting you wait on him, and says he's buying all that lingerie for his wife. What was his name?"

"Clive Hardy. He may be a little eccentric, but he's harmless."

Helen shook her head. "Get a clue, honey. You're such an innocent."

"But this letter is inventive, not crude," Annie protested. Just then a movement from the corner of her eye made her turn to confront John Riley, who was standing to one side, obviously listening.

"I'm interrupting, aren't I?" the local gallery owner asked.

Wondering how long he'd been standing there and how much he'd overheard, Annie snatched her letter back from Nick and indicated a chair. Riley came in so often that she figured he was either a true coffee junkie or he had the hots for Helen, which would be no surprise, since her friend was a brainy blond bombshell. With his mahogany hair, green eyes and broad shoulders, Riley was no slouch himself.

"No biggie," Annie said as she slid out of her seat. "I was on my way out, anyway."

She hoped that her fickle friend would take the hint and invest herself in someone who seemed to know what he wanted. The overly particular Helen went through boyfriends almost as fast as Nick went through women—though she probably averaged three strikes to his one.

Riley seemed surprised that she was leaving. "You're in some hurry tonight."

Picking up her coffee, she joked, "I've got a hot date waiting for me."

Easier than having to explain that she was eager to get home to a cat.

"Have a good one."

Streetlights glowed bright against the dark, moonless night as Annie set off on foot up Milwaukee Avenue, drinking her coffee. As usual, she glanced in the store windows that lined the first few blocks, mentally critiquing the displays.

Too conservative…too kitschy…too avant garde. None touched her or sparked her imagination.

Being a city person, she was used to walking, and quite enjoyed her "commute," especially after being cooped up in the store all day. And the near mile to and from work helped to keep her in shape. Walking also gave her quiet time to think.

Taking another sip of the coffee, she considered her friends' reactions to the anonymous letter. Maybe she shouldn't have shared it with Nick and Helen, though she trusted no one more.

Helen had only reflected a worry that she herself already had about the letter, Annie admitted. Although actually the youngest of the three, Helen had always seemed older than her age and tended to mother her and Nick. In a freaky, intellectual sort of way, that was. On the other hand, Nick hadn't seemed in the least worried. Then again, not much ever seemed to trouble Nicholas Novak.

Halfway home, Annie was taking her usual shortcut under the elevated tracks when a train rumbled overhead. She hurried but couldn't avoid the grit that filtered down on her as the train sped by.

"Great," she muttered, pausing to brush the loose particles from her hair and clothing.

That's when she heard it—a noise from somewhere behind her. But when she turned, she could see nothing amiss. Only dark and more dark. She hurried off, anyway.

No matter how fast she walked, she couldn't leave

behind the sensation of someone lurking behind her. The impression stuck to her like glue.

Her pulse skittered. Her mouth went dry. Her racing heartbeat rushed through her ears.

Hurrying, she tripped over something she couldn't see, felt the warmth of her coffee slosh over her hand. Dropping the cup, she practically ran toward the light ahead.

She was never so glad to set foot on her street.

Out of breath, she was relieved when an old couple, accompanied by a middle-aged, fit-looking man, left one of the remaining bungalows in the area. She slowed and turned and, walking backward, stared into the darkness she had left, but no danger followed.

Her imagination?

Undoubtedly her unease had been prompted by the letter and Helen's reaction to it, Annie told herself. She was safe.

Still reassuring herself, she tried not to let her hand shake when she unlocked her door and let herself into her loft—or what would be her loft if she ever got the financing to renovate the former manufacturing building that she'd bought with her inheritance. City inspectors had put their seal on the place so that she could live there, but the space was just that. Space. Potential. Not like a real home at all…except for Rock.

"Hey, my big boy, did you miss me?" she asked, as the still-scruffy orange-and-white cat wound himself around her ankles. "I'll bet you're hungry, aren't you?"

Feeding him gave her back a sense of normalcy. As usual, he couldn't decide which he wanted more—

food or her attention. She gave him both together. Running her hand down his back and up his tail as he ate made her feel better.

As did a microwaved dinner and an abbreviated shower, after which she tried to get into one of the romance novels that sat in a stack next to her bed. Too tired. Her eyes didn't want to focus on the written page.

So instead she watched some television, horizontal-style, with a purring Rock on her chest.

Then the television slowly began to blur…

She awoke to darkness but for the blue glow emanating from the TV. Disoriented, she lay there, feeling for the remote control device. Her hand encountered it with a force that sent it skidding over the bed and onto the floor.

"Damn!"

Hanging over the mattress, she felt for the remote, but instead of finding it, her hand brushed fur. The cat was cowering under the bed.

"Rock, come out here."

But the cat crawled farther underneath.

"Rock, sweetheart, what's wrong?"

He growled in answer.

The short hairs on the back of Annie's neck stood at attention. He never acted like this. She'd never heard him growl before. What the hell was going on?

She whipped straight up and peered around, the only light the blue glow from the screen. Her heart thundering, she could hardly swallow.

There it was, that creepy feeling again.

Slipping off the bed, she crossed to the door.

Locked. She checked the windows. Locked. But Rock was still freaked, still hiding.

Annie picked up the phone and used speed dial. Helen's recorded voice answered. She hung up and tried Nick. No answer at all. What to do?

Call the police? And tell them what? Because her cat was freaked, so was she?

She hesitated, then hit the third number and counted the rings. One...two...

"Yeah," a male voice growled from the other end.

"It's Annie Wilder," she said with a gasp. "I know it's the middle of the night, but I'm taking you at your word—you said if I needed *anything* I should call."

2

THROUGH SLEEP-HEAVY EYES, Nate glanced at the glowing numbers of his bedside digital clock and groaned. Nearly four-thirty in the morning.

"Nathaniel, are you there?" asked the shaky voice over his cell phone. "I—I did get the right number, didn't I? This *is* Nathaniel Bishop, right?"

His brain awakening slowly, Nate finally registered the voice. "Annie? Is that you?"

"Yeah, it's me."

Could she really be at her shop this late? he wondered. "What's wrong?"

Certain that she wouldn't call him about a washer or a bad outlet or a broken light fixture in the middle of the night, he forced himself fully awake.

"Maybe nothing, I don't know, but Rock is freaked and so am I. Helen's voice mail is taking her calls and I can't get hold of Nick and I just didn't know who else to talk to."

She jumbled the words together as if she had a time limit to get them out.

"Whoa. Slow down," Nate said, visualizing panic widening her big gray eyes and pulling at her delicate, heart-shaped face. "So your cat is freaked. Why?"

"I—I don't know. But he's under the bed…uh, hi,

Rock. He just jumped up beside me. And he's purring. He seems okay now."

"And what about you?"

"I guess I'm still a little freaked," Annie admitted. "The letter got me started, then I imagined that someone was following me home, and then I wake up in the middle of the night to find the cat under the bed, growling. I just needed someone to talk to is all."

Finally, she was starting to make sense, Nate thought, swinging his bare legs over the bed. "Does your cat usually growl?"

"Never. Not that I've heard."

He rose and headed for the bathroom. "Give me your address and I'll come over and check things out for you."

"You don't have to do that. Just talking to you helped."

He could hear the lie in her words.

"Your address, Annie."

Relief sighed through her voice as she gave it to him. "It's a big, squat, two-story brown brick, unrenovated building," she clarified, "part of the old manufacturing district."

"I'll be there as fast as I can. Don't answer the door to anyone but me. When I get to your place, I'll call you on the cell phone to let you know I'm outside."

"All right. Thanks. I owe you."

"My pleasure, Annie."

He'd been waiting for an opportunity like this for months.

ANNIE HAD DRESSED in jeans and a gray silk shirt, and had just pulled back her hair into an off-center ponytail that trailed over her shoulder when the phone rang a little after five. Relieved, she picked up the receiver.

"I'm riding up your block now."

"I'll meet you at the door." She hung up and told Rock, "A friend is here. No need to hide under the bed."

Listening for a car, she heard an angry buzz instead. And when she opened the door, she simply gaped as Nathaniel Bishop rode up on a black-and-red Harley. He dismounted and removed his helmet to reveal dark hair tossed over his forehead. Then he came toward her, a somewhat intriguing and yet threatening figure.

She blinked and adjusted her glasses, but the apparition in black leather didn't disappear.

"Are you going to stand there or let me in?" he asked.

"In." She stepped back to let him pass, then locked up and leaned against the door. She couldn't stop staring. "I wasn't expecting..." She waved her hand to indicate his surprising alter ego.

"I guess not." He grinned. "Up until now you've only seen my business persona."

"Clark Kent," she agreed.

He laughed. "Try Nate," he replied, studying her face. "You seem to be feeling better."

"Actually, I'm feeling a little foolish."

She glanced over to her bed in the middle of the two-story space. Rock stared at the newcomer for a moment before disappearing back under her bed.

"Ro-o-ck," she called, to no avail. And when the

cat didn't reappear, she told Nate, "He's shy of strangers. Who knows what happened to him out on the street?"

"That's understandable. Well, since I'm here, it won't hurt for me to check things out for you."

Nate released a big flashlight from a loop at his waist and started a tour of the place.

Annie cringed. She took such care with Annie's Attic, but the new business had been so all consuming that she'd done virtually nothing with her new home—a big, empty, cold-looking space softened only by her bed and a sitting area with plush couches and chairs. Her few accessories consisted of a dozen fancy pillows, souvenirs from flea markets and vacations and estate sales. In addition, she had a functional kitchen and functional bath and that was that.

Though she couldn't afford to renovate at this time, she could certainly add her own touch to the place, make it more interesting. Only half of the building rose the full two stories. The other half had a second floor, filled with treasures from an estate sale that were still mostly in boxes. Maybe she'd better start digging stuff out.

She followed Nate at a distance. His flashlight beam swept every dark corner. Suddenly something scurrying along the back wall made her yelp.

"A rat!" she squeaked, as it found a space in the outside wall and squeezed through.

"Aha, mystery solved." Nate grabbed a dishcloth and hurried to stuff it in the hole. "Rock was hiding under the bed because he's afraid of a little rodent."

"Me, too! At least it's gone now."

"You'll have to bring an exterminator in tomorrow

to get rid of any other unwanted guests and to seal up any entrances you don't know about. And while you're at it, you need a security system protecting this place."

Though she'd never felt unsafe before, Annie admitted that a security system wouldn't be amiss. "I'll dig through the yellow pages first thing."

"I had to find both for my building when I renovated it," Nate said. "And I still use the exterminator, of course. When I get to the office, I'll get you the contact information for both businesses."

"I owe you big," she said gratefully.

"How about a *big* breakfast, then? I'm starving."

She glanced at the kitchen area. "Cold cereal?"

Nate gave her a look that sent shivers to her toes. "You need to stop working so hard, and take care of yourself." He looked around. "You wouldn't own a helmet?"

"Plastic foam. Bike-style."

"It'll have to do this time." He sounded as if he had ideas for future times, as well. "Get a jacket or sweater while you're at it."

A few minutes later, Annie was perched behind Nate on his Harley and flying to who knew where. With her arms around his middle and her thighs spread around his, she was a bit giddy and totally into the moment, and she didn't care where they were heading.

They landed at a small breakfast place that had opened at 5:00 a.m. Eggxactly was a narrow space with a long counter and tables that were already half-filled. Around the room, shelves held old toasters and waffle irons and egg poachers as part of the decor.

"It's perfect," Annie said, feeling right at home as she slid into a booth.

"And the food is even better."

He was right. Though dawn was still an hour away, she ate with appetite—stuffed French toast, filet benedict, roasted breakfast potatoes.

Before sitting down to eat, Nate had removed the leather jacket that had been zipped to his pants. Beneath, he wore a blue silk T-shirt a shade darker than his eyes. Though he was tall, he wasn't a big man. Not broad. But he had respectable musculature. With unexpected fascination, Annie watched his biceps flex as he lifted the fork to his mouth.

Suddenly, she said, "You're so unexpected."

"The Clark Kent thing?"

She shrugged. "I didn't have a clue."

"You thought I was an uptight businessman."

"Not uptight," she hedged, remembering her critical assessment of him the day before.

"Boring, then. Don't deny it. I am when I'm working, because that's what most people expect. But we all lead at least two lives, don't we?"

"Not necessarily."

"Then we want to—we fantasize about it," he insisted. "It's human nature. We have one face for public, another for private." Nate studied her for a moment before adding, "I wonder what your private face is like."

"You're looking at it."

"Am I?"

She shifted uncomfortably. "What you see is what you get. Sorry to disappoint you."

"Who said I was disappointed?"

Nate locked gazes with her and wouldn't let go. Heat curled around her middle and she suddenly went light-headed. She had a mouthful of food but no will to swallow. Just as the tension sparked between them to an unbearable degree, he looked away and took a slug of coffee.

"Why Annie's Attic?"

"Fantasy. People like it." Then she thought of her detractors. The picket line that had formed outside her door the day after her grand opening. "Well, most people."

"And you?"

"I wanted to do something creative and fun from the moment I figured out that I had talent. Unfortunately, I thought a career in advertising would give me both. Instead, I ended up with hard-to-please clients who thought they knew 'creative' better than I did. What a headache."

"So that prompted you to open your own business."

"No. Actually, Nick did. He and Helen and I hung out together in college and shared our dreams. Then we graduated and all got great-paying jobs on the fast track to misery. One day, Nick put it to us. Quit our jobs and start our own businesses. Helen and I didn't take him seriously until he showed us the listing for your building, along with his resignation—he'd been shooting video footage for news shows at a network-affiliated television station, but he quit, just like that."

"So you made a pact? The Three Musketeers?"

She nodded. "Helen quit her job as a corporate Webmistress and I said goodbye to advertising. We vowed to support each other no matter what."

"Have you ever regretted giving up a paycheck?"

"No," Annie said honestly. "Even the few problems I've had with those who don't approve of the store couldn't ruin it for me."

The sky was lightening on the horizon when they left the restaurant. Annie couldn't remember the last time she'd been out and about this early.

Rather than heading back to her place, however, Nate rode straight toward the lake along the deserted streets. The city was just awakening.

More exhilarated than she'd been in years, Annie didn't object. Her face to the wind, she found renewed enjoyment in the concept of freedom. Her front to his back, her nerve endings a-tingle with the intimate contact, she came alive as she hadn't truly been for what seemed like a lifetime.

For Nate…not for Nathaniel. Nathaniel *was* boring, even if she wouldn't say so to him. Nate was anything but. Nate was every girl's fantasy. Well, this girl's, anyway. Nate Bishop, the modern-day version of a knight in shining armor come to save a maiden in distress.

Annie closed her eyes.

He shot through the mist on a black charger. Threatened by a dragon—a dragon that had certain ratlike features—she reached up toward her black knight.

Her heart thudded when he lifted her away from danger and onto his faithful steed. They rode together, her back to his front.

One gloved hand traced a line from her throat to the valley between her breasts and down to her belly, where heat sizzled in concentric circles until she was consumed....

Gasping at the intensity of the fantasy, Annie opened her eyes as Nate braked to a stop.

They were in one of the few wooded areas along Chicago's Lake Michigan shoreline, giving them a measure of privacy. She wondered if it was even legal for him to have driven up here—they were off pavement and on a gravel road in a grassy area. Before them, golden-pink light streamed across the water as the sun peeked over the horizon.

Her heart thudding in truth, Annie reluctantly released Nate and dismounted, awed by the spectacular beauty of the moment as the sun seemed to launch itself suddenly from the lake. Her breath caught in her throat and she removed her helmet. Nate dismounted and removed his helmet as well, tossing it on the grass.

Spring flowers covered a nearby patch of ground and he stooped to pluck a yellow primrose. Then he turned toward her and stepped close enough to kiss her.

"How beautiful," she whispered.

But it was his mouth rather than the sunrise at which she now stared. Yes, indeed, quite a beautiful mouth, she thought, recognizing the sensuality that she had only guessed at the day before in her store. More than anything, Annie wanted to feel those lips against hers.

"Yes, beautiful." Nate set the flower in her hair, tucking it in the band holding her ponytail in place. "Flowers suit you." He brushed stray wisps of hair from her cheek and straightened her glasses.

And then he kissed her.

The helmet slipped from her suddenly lifeless fingers.

Mouth covering hers, Nate moved in closer, caught her low under her buttocks and pulled her up and into him. Without hesitation, she wrapped her arms around his neck as he opened her mouth and explored the sensitive flesh inside with a soft, sexy tongue. Unable to help herself, she slipped one leg up his and wrapped it around his thigh. Still invading her mouth, he hiked her up again and nudged her other thigh higher until both of her legs were wrapped around him.

Holding her weight, he spun around in circles until the world seemed to whirl past them in a rush, until Annie was giddy with the sensation.

Then the kiss ended and the world toppled and she found herself flat on her back in the grass, Nate stretched half over her, his weight making her catch her breath even as the sunrise had. Even through the leather, she felt the length and breadth of his desire for her and couldn't help but respond. Heat flushed along her nerves, a pulsing sensation that she couldn't ignore. But even though his eyes were heavy-lidded—sexy bedroom eyes, she mused—Nate didn't press her to go further. Which surprised her.

As Nate stared down at her, a smile suddenly quirked his lips, deepening the cleft in his chin and making him even better looking, if that were possible. Her heart began to thud.

Squirming inwardly, she murmured, "What?"

"What?" he echoed.

"The smile."

"A reason? Do I need one?"

"It makes you seem so...I don't know..."

"Relaxed?"

Annie couldn't help herself. His smile was contagious, and suddenly she was grinning back at him. "Okay, that's a good word."

A *safe* word.

"Why shouldn't I be relaxed? I'm with *you.*"

And with that, Nate rolled over on his back, reached out and found her hand and possessively threaded his fingers through hers. They lay there in silence as morning touched Annie in a way it never had before. Gazing out at Lake Michigan, she lost herself in the golden blush that hung over the horizon as the sun blossomed and tinged everything in its reach with a glow as soft and sparkling as fairy dust.

A voice in her head suddenly intruded, suggesting that maybe the illusion of fairy dust was brought about by smudges on her glasses.

Annie shook away the cynical thought. He was with *her* and that made him smile.

She'd never heard that line before, her negative side thought.

If it was a line, her more positive self countered.

But, as usual, the cynic won, and Annie quickly grew restless, anxious to be alone where she could think things through. She extricated her hand and sat straight up and, through eyes that weren't filled with stardust, realized that morning had broken and it was just another day. She removed her glasses and, using the edge of her jacket, cleared the smudges made by his cheek.

"Maybe we should be getting back," Annie said

matter-of-factly, making a mental list of the things she needed to tackle. "I have that exterminator to contact."

"Right."

She started to rise, but Nate beat her to it and held out his hand. Reluctantly, she let him help her to her feet, and was relieved that he didn't try to get closer. Bad enough that she'd have to hang on to him on the cycle.

During the ride back, she blanked her mind. No need to replay a perfect morning and torture herself with what probably had been a once-in-a-lifetime experience. After all, "Nate" might never appear in her life again.

It wasn't until they were approaching the six corners that she realized he was taking her to Annie's Attic rather than home. No problem. Rock was fed and she did have that paperwork to finish. Besides, he could get those numbers for her. Finding an exterminator was definitely a priority. No way was she going to willingly share her new digs with uninvited rodents.

Preoccupied, she was startled when Nate stiffened and said, "Damn!" and brought the cycle to an abrupt stop.

"What's wrong?"

They were in front of Annie's Attic, and the source of his anger was immediately apparent. Her stomach twisted.

Someone had painted TRASH in big red letters across her display window.

3

"WHAT A SWELL WAY to start my morning. What the heck is your security guard doing, anyway?" a frustrated Annie lashed out. "Sleeping on the job?"

"Harry Burdock makes the rounds at four different buildings in this area twice a night," Nate said, keeping his tone reasonable. "And he only works until 6:00 a.m., so this could have happened after he was off duty."

He was right, of course. Annie sighed. What a mess. The last time it had been eggs smeared all over her display window. Now it was paint.

"Maybe I should've trained as a cleanup expert," she muttered.

"With two of us at it—"

"No! This is my problem. *I* will fix it."

"I don't mind. It is my building."

"But it's *my* business," she stubbornly insisted.

Nate stared at her. Then, as if realizing she wasn't going to budge, he nodded. For a moment she thought he might come closer, might kiss her again, but then probably thought better of the impulse, because he backed off, spine stiff and expression oddly neutral. The pulse that jagged through her for a few seconds settled right down.

He was looking a lot more like Nathaniel than

Nate, she thought with surprise and a vague sense of disappointment.

He said, "I'll talk to you later, then."

"No, wait, Nate." What some jerk had done wasn't his fault, and she shouldn't take it out on him. "Thanks, again. Really. For everything."

He softened back into Nate. "Anytime."

Annie watched him mount the Harley and ride off, and a part of her wished that she could go with him. But a bigger part of her was highly ticked when she looked back at the scarlet letters.

Morality was in the mind of the beholder, Annie thought. She found lots of things immoral—poverty, abuse, violence...desecrating other people's property! But there was nothing immoral about the fantasies she sold. Fantasies were a natural inclination, a part of human nature, just as were the sexual encounters that might be prompted by those very fantasies.

Well, sex was part of most people's lives, anyway.

Disgusted, she unlocked the shop and went inside, where she took off her bike helmet.

A quick glance into the mirror reminded her of the flower Nate had tucked into her hair. Now it was woefully crushed. Saddened, she removed it, but she just couldn't throw it away. Instead, she got a glass, filled it with water and tucked the flower inside.

Leaving it on her desk as a reminder of the *good* part of the morning, she headed into the storage area to get what she needed to clean up the mess. Since she did her own displays and ads, she was well armed to deal with paint. She grabbed a small can of paint thinner and a handful of old rags and marched back outside.

No doubt the culprit thought she was some kind of sexpert, she groused to herself as, with a fury, she attacked the latest desecration of her establishment. Well, if that was the problem, the joke was on whoever had done this.

Quickly, she obliterated the damning letters, if not the brilliant color. The faster she wiped, the faster the bright red smear spread across the glass.

And to her horror, people on their way to the rapid transit station stopped to watch and whisper.

Head buzzing a bit from the fumes, she wiped harder and faster, turning the rags to use every inch of cloth. The red began to disappear from the window, but she could still see a faint outline where the letters had been. And, she was certain, so could the small crowd that had formed behind her back.

A row of business suits reflected in the plate glass, as did a long, black car that pulled up and stopped at the curb. Annie glanced over her shoulder as an electric window whined and lowered. Alderman Vincent Zavadinski glared out at her, his silver-shot beetle brows pulling into a straight line.

Annie remembered seeing him outside the window the evening before. Red-streaked rags in equally red-streaked hands, she went straight for the car, the crowd parting around her like the Red Sea. The look of satisfaction settling on the man's face made her *see* red, too.

"Alderman, interested in spicing up your personal life?" she asked sweetly.

Color flushed Zavadinski's full cheeks and clashed with the silver-threaded blond hair slicked back from a high forehead. "Hardly."

"Then you approve of what happened here."

"What's not to approve? Someone pinned you and your business, Miss Wilder. Someone had the guts to speak up with the truth."

"Truth?" she echoed. "Guts? Sneaking around in the middle of the night with a can of paint takes guts? Whoever did this is a coward. And you can tell him I said so."

"M-me?" he sputtered. "You think *I* had something to do with defacing private property?"

Annie narrowed her gaze on his increasingly ruddy face. "No, of course not. You just happened along. You stopped to join the other gawkers."

"I was concerned that someone was *hurt.*"

Hurt....

A shudder ran through Annie. Paint was a pretty impotent weapon. But she hadn't forgotten the fear that had frozen her insides when she'd thought she was being followed the night before.

What if she had been? What if it hadn't been her imagination, after all?

Renewed fear, added to anger, fired her up. Annie could hardly keep from shaking as she asked, "That wasn't some kind of threat, was it, Alderman Zavadinski?" in a voice loud enough for everyone to hear. "You wouldn't physically threaten a woman—a woman running a legal business—in front of witnesses, would you?"

If looks could kill... The alderman withdrew and the electric window whined upward, effectively shutting her out.

"Show's over, folks," Annie told the spectators as she straightened. Her insides were tumbling, but she was determined not to show it. "Come on back when we open at ten." They were already moving off, probably never to return, but she continued her spiel. "Annie's Attic is open for business six days a week, ten until seven, except for Sundays, when we're open noon to five. We're closed on Mondays."

Realizing she was alone once more, Annie suddenly felt deflated. She glanced back at her handiwork. A ghostly TRASH still mocked her.

Determined to eradicate the reminder of mean-spiritedness, she went inside and found a roll of paper towels and window cleaner, plus a razor blade that she could use to scrape away the remains of the paint.

Around nine-thirty, Gloria Delgado reported for work, early as usual, as Annie was polishing the now-clean window to a luster.

Today the Hispanic woman wore her mass of hair up, though several glossy, blue-black curls dangled over the shoulders of her bright orange jacket. A skimpy purple top, lime-green miniskirt and purple platform shoes and shoulder bag completed the eye-popping outfit. The store's assistant manager certainly had her own style, the reason Annie had hired her. She'd never been sorry—Gloria related well to the trend-conscious younger neighborhood women who came into Annie's Attic to shop.

"What's going on, boss? The window washers on strike or something?"

"More like the neighborhood," Annie muttered. As she went back into the store, Gloria following closely, she explained what had happened.

Outraged, Gloria stuck a fist on one full hip and waved her other index finger in the air as she said,

"You know, I'm gonna tell my cousin Julio to have his boys keep an eye on the place at night."

As usual, Gloria acted as if she had a vested interest in the business, which in a way she did, Annie supposed, since the other woman had been by her side since day one. But knowing Julio and his boys were part of a local gang, Annie figured she didn't need them involved.

"Don't tell your cousin anything!" Realizing she sounded too harsh, Annie muttered, "I mean, it was only paint." She was trying not to think of it as a warning.

"They're okay, you know, Julio and his boys," Gloria argued. "They're just regular guys." Then, as if realizing that argument wouldn't convince anyone, she shrugged her shoulders. "Well, you change your mind, you say the word."

"Thanks for the thought, Gloria. I know you mean well."

"We gotta stick together, you and me. You gave me a chance to make something of myself here, and not at no minimum wage job, neither. I don't want this business run outta the neighborhood because some jerks with no *cajones* have nothing better to do than make trouble."

Who needed Julio and his pals? If those *cajone*less jerks had any brains, they would stay out of dark alleys when Gloria Delgado was around. She was the toughest woman Annie had ever known.

"Annie's Attic won't be run out of anywhere, Gloria. I promise I won't cave."

A little false bravado made Annie feel better. She left her assistant in the shop with its colors and scents and fabrics meant to bring nothing but joy to people's lives, while she went back into the janitor's closet behind all the stores to trash the rags and empty thinner can and clean the paint from her hands. She was just about through when she felt a presence behind her.

Heart hammering, Annie whipped around to find Nate—correction, Nathaniel, because he was wearing one of his expensive suits, custom white shirts and blah ties—standing in the doorway.

NATE WATCHED ANNIE'S FACE flood with sensuous color, and fought the urge to pull her into his arms, pin her at the sink and take her right there. Not that she looked as if she wanted to be taken. She simply seemed...uncomfortable.

"What are *you* doing here?"

And not exactly happy to see him, Nate thought. "My offices are here, remember."

"Upstairs."

"I can't check on my own building?"

Though it was the tenant who held his interest at the moment. And now that he'd found a way to get to her, he wasn't about to do a disappearing act.

Her discomfort growing before his eyes, Annie shrugged. "I—I guess you can do whatever you want in your own building. You just startled me."

He wondered. She seemed uneasy with *him.*

"I thought you would want this." He held out a card. "The exterminator's number." When she looked blank, he said, "The rat?"

"Oh. Right. I can think of more than one rat I'd like exterminated!"

Avoiding his fingers, she took the card from him gingerly, glanced at it and tucked it into a back pocket of her jeans.

An awkward silence hung between them as Nate waited for her to follow up. A thank-you might be in order, though he would prefer a "nice to see you again." Which he obviously wasn't going to hear.

"I had a great time with you this morning," Nate said, trying to keep it casual. Trying to keep from scaring her. He could see the pulse flutter in her throat. He could almost taste it. Being this close to her and not being able to touch her was driving him crazy. "I mean...considering the reason you called."

"You were something of a distraction," she admitted, averting her eyes.

Her sudden shyness made him want her. Here. Now. On the damn janitor's sink. Thinking about it tightened his groin so that he had to shift his stance.

"I'd like to distract you some more," Nate admitted. He knew he had to be careful how he handled her. She was like a butterfly ready to spring from her cocoon, and he meant to be there when it happened—but he knew that he would be only if he was very, very careful. "How about over dinner? You close shop at seven, and that's about the time I get out of a late meeting with some investors. I could make reservations at Chic for seven-thirty."

"Chic?"

Her distressed expression surprised him. "You don't like French food?"

"It's not that. Chic is, um, kind of upscale."

Annie indicated her outfit, the same jeans and silk shirt she'd had on when he'd picked her up that morning. She looked good to him—good enough to eat—but he supposed she would feel as if she were too casually dressed.

"I can make it later," he said, not caring about the hour, just as long as he could spend some time with her. "Give you time to change. I'll pick you up at home."

"To tell you the truth," Annie said with a forced smile, "Chic really isn't my style."

He gazed into her eyes, but she kept herself closed off from him.

"Then *you* pick the restaurant."

"I didn't get much sleep last night...."

This was becoming painful. How many ways did she have to say no before he got it through his thick head that she wasn't going to have dinner with him?

So he would have to put his plans on hold, look for a different, more enticing opening. He tamped down his frustration.

"Some other night then," he promised, keeping his voice even.

"Sure. Maybe."

Okay, so she didn't want to go out with him again *ever.* But why not? Determined to change her mind, Nate smiled at Annie through clenched teeth. She'd seemed immune to his charms for months, but now he knew that she *wasn't* truly impervious to him. The kiss had proved that. So what was the problem?

Trying to pick up that connection they'd made earlier, he said, "And about the security guard—Burdock said everything was fine when he checked the building at five. So someone messed with your window after that. I'm going to have him spend less time at the other buildings and more here. I'll tell him to keep an eye on Annie's Attic specifically."

"You don't need to do that."

But Nate could see that he did. Annie had softened just a bit. And now the expression in her eyes was more confused than closed. So he'd found the approach he needed. He'd been waiting too long for his opportunity to get close to her to let any opening pass him by.

If making Annie Wilder feel protected would do the trick, then he was on it.

BY THE TIME ANNIE wandered back into the shop, Gloria was finishing with a customer. Good thing, or she might have questions about the heightened color in her boss's cheeks. After Nathaniel left, Annie had caught a glimpse of herself in a mirror and been startled by the apparition staring back. Though she'd easily steeled herself against Nathaniel, she had found herself thinking about Nate.

Her hands were feeling a little raw from the chemicals and the scrubbing, so she opened a bottle of massage oil meant for more delicate areas, and slathered it on. The oil itself was immediately absorbed into her skin, but the soft honeysuckle scent lingered.

She walked through the French Quarter of New Orleans. Honeysuckle hung heavy on the hot night air. Perspiration dotted her body beneath her clothing and she longed for a tall, cool drink.

A burbling fountain called to her. She followed its enticing sound into a courtyard. Dipping her hand into the water, she brought a palmful to her neck and let the cool liquid trickle between her breasts.

"Can I help?" he asked. A voice thick with promise seduced her from the shadows....

"I'm hot," she whispered. "So very, very hot."

"Then take off your clothes. I won't mind."

She hesitated only a second, then began undoing the pearl buttons on her dress....

A chill hit her skin and Annie came back to the present with a start. Horrified, she realized she'd actually unbuttoned the front of her silk shirt. The air-conditioning had pebbled the sensitive skin of her breasts. But her back was to the main part of the store and, thankfully, no one was standing at the window.

Quickly, she buttoned back up before anyone strolled by.

Nothing like this had ever happened to her before. What had she been thinking?

A little strung out, she was relieved when the customer left a few minutes later.

"I'm going to get some coffee," she told Gloria. "Want something?"

"Nah, you go ahead. Chill a little, huh?" Gloria arched a perfectly shaped dark brow. "Hmm, considering how strung out you've been, maybe you'd better get a decaf."

Snorting at Gloria's acerbic observation, Annie left for Helen's Cybercafé.

A late riser, Nick had just arrived and was having his so-called breakfast, coffee and a muffin. Ordering a cappuccino, Annie joined Nick and Helen, and shared her latest trauma with her best friends.

"So you really think the alderman is behind this?" Helen asked.

"I can't be sure, since there were no witnesses. But

it's awfully coincidental that I saw him outside the store last night and then he happened by this morning. I have a feeling he's responsible, all right, even if he didn't do the dirty deed himself."

"Maybe we can convince Nick to install a SpyCam just in case whoever it was returns to the scene of the crime."

"Say the word," Nick agreed, stuffing half a muffin into his mouth.

Just the word *spycam* gave her a shiver. She'd never been one for invading anyone's privacy, and she could only imagine what they might catch on tape if she agreed.

"I don't think that's really necessary," she said. "Nathaniel is basically pulling the security guard off his regular route to keep an eye on the building."

"Our landlord already knows? What did he do?" Helen asked. "Arrive while you were removing the paint?"

"Uh, not exactly. He was dropping me off at the store. Rather, Nate was."

Helen sat up straight at that. "I think a more thorough explanation is called for here."

"Yeah, spill," Nick ordered.

So spill she did. Everything from her spooky walk home the night before, to Nate's finding the rat and buying her breakfast, to seeing the scarlet letters painted across her display window. Everything but the interlude at the lakefront. Everything but the kiss that now had her a little freaked out.

"So Nate's your knight in shining armor," Nick said.

Remembering the fantasy she'd had of Nate fighting the rat-dragon, Annie laughed. "I guess you could call him that." *Among other things.*

"I'd call it a little weird," Helen objected. "Why in the world would a landlord of a business show up to rescue a tenant at home?"

Nick poked her with his elbow. "Don't be a dunce. Obviously, he has ulterior motives."

"Exactly!"

Her cheeks suddenly seared with heat, Annie protested, "Stop making it sound so...so serious!"

"It's high time you got serious about someone," Nick said.

Not wanting to rehash her disastrous relationship with Alan Cooper, and the caution with which she'd viewed the handful of men she'd dated over the past several years, she said, "Look who's talking."

"You're not like Helen and me, Annie. You have no interest in playing the field. You're a one-man woman. You just picked the wrong one first time around. We all make mistakes. Until now, I despaired of your ever being interested in any guy ever again. It's about time."

Nick and Helen were the only ones who understood how much she'd cared for Alan and how his betrayal had devastated her. Nate was the first man who really interested her on more than a surface level since. That Helen didn't say anything encouraging unnerved Annie a bit. She could tell her friend was biting her tongue to keep from adding her two cents worth.

"Look, don't read anything into it, okay, Nick? You're jumping the gun here."

"Then you're not interested in Nathaniel Bishop?"

"No," she said honestly.

She wasn't. Not Nathaniel. But Nate could raise her blood pressure and twist her insides into a knot. He could make her imagine being a damsel in distress...or a wanton.

Helen was staring at her speculatively. "Something's fishy here."

"I don't smell anything," Annie said lightly, trying to rise until Helen caught her arm in a firm grip.

"You're not going anywhere until I get every last detail. You know, the ones you left out."

"I should be getting back to the store," Annie protested as she reluctantly settled back into the chair. "It's nearly lunch hour."

"Which Gloria is perfectly capable of handling."

Annie groaned, wanting to smack her forehead against the table. She knew that tone. Helen, who for some reason chose to mother her, was not going to let it go.

"You know she won't give up," Nick said, echoing Annie's thoughts. He was sitting back, grinning devilishly, enjoying her discomfort. "So you might as well make it easy on yourself."

"All right. I give. We kissed."

"You and Nathaniel?"

"Me and Nate. We watched the sun come up over the lake and kissed. That's it."

"No slap and tickle?"

Annie glowered at Nick. "I'm not into hooking up, as you well know. One kiss." One stomach-clenching, world-whirling, mind-shattering kiss. "Period."

Her friends didn't have to know that she'd been so aroused that she might have done something foolish, given the chance. That even now she couldn't stop Nate from entering her fantasies.

"What I don't understand is why you make the distinction," Helen said. "No, you didn't kiss Nathaniel, but yes, you did kiss Nate. They're the same guy."

"No, not really. Nathaniel is all business. A little uptight." Annie grimaced. "He's kind of boring. But Nate...he's—"

"The heroic fantasy," Nick supplied.

"Exactly."

"A rogue on wheels."

"Right."

"A ravisher of fair maidens."

"Have you been into Annie's romance novels again?" Helen asked.

Nick pretended to be wounded. "Just trying to keep my fingers on the pulse of fresh young womanhood."

"Okay!" Annie popped up out of her chair and silently challenged Helen to try to stop her. "I'm outta here."

This time her friend let her go. But as Annie backed away from the table, Helen's expression was speculative and curiously disapproving.

Sending a frisson of unease up Annie's spine.

Not that she had time to dwell on it. Back at the shop, Gloria was swamped with lunchtime customers. And Annie was happy to dive right in and lend a hand.

The shop was busier than normal. Annie overheard mention of Zavadinski's name at one point, and realized the neighborhood must be abuzz with news of the face-off that morning.

Then traffic slowed for a while and, after Gloria took a break, Annie wandered back to her office and the computer.

Helen had created a Website for her. Business was picking up there, as well. Printing a half-dozen orders and filling them, Annie decided to wait until the next day to take them to the post office. Maybe more orders would come in by then and she could save herself a trip.

The shop had gotten busy again—crowded even, Annie noted with amazement. She recognized several women who'd been spectators that morning. Whoever had said bad publicity was better than none probably had a point.

By closing time, she was exhausted, and still customers remained. She and Gloria took care of every last one before calling it a day.

Then, as usual, after the final count from the cash register, Gloria took the day's receipts to the night drop at the bank across the street.

And Annie turned to the window display.

WHICH ARTICLE OF CLOTHING would be next? he wondered.

He watched, entranced, as she finished pulling the sweater off the female mannequin and added it to the growing pile of discarded clothing. Then she leaned over the window display and rolled the die, just as if she were playing the game herself. She moved a piece several spaces forward on the board.

Which one? His groin tightened. *The bra. Let it be the bra.*

Then he imagined her braless. What kind of breasts did she have? he wondered. Firm or soft? Nipples large or tight little buds?

Hard just thinking about it, he rubbed himself discreetly. Not enough to draw attention even if a passerby were to look in the shadows of the doorway.

Just enough to start the electric haze, that thick, soupy state of mind that made it difficult to concentrate but, oh, so easy to feel....

But when she reached over and removed one of the male mannequin's socks, he instantly deflated with disappointment.

"Damn!"

He would just have to wait for the real thing.

4

ANNIE HAD THAT FEELING again, the same one that had spurred her home so fast the night before. It had started while she'd been working on the window display—that edgy sensation of being watched.

But when she'd turned her attention to what lay beyond the plate glass, the street had mocked her with its emptiness. The rush hour was over. People were home eating dinner or perhaps at restaurants. Everyone but her.

Still she couldn't rid herself of that creepy sensation that made her skin prickle.

Her imagination, she tried to tell herself again.

But was it?

A shiver shot through her as she switched off the lights, set the alarms and prepared to leave.

Gradually, the feeling lessened a bit, and jacket on, key ring in hand, she shot out onto the sidewalk planning to make a fast getaway. But the lock defied her and she fumbled the keys and the back of her neck crawled until, finally, the key penetrated the lock successfully.

The door was secured.

Taking a shaky breath of relief and turning for home, Annie ran smack into a big body.

"A-ah!" she yelped, jumping back.

"Sorry to scare you, miss. You all right?"

Harry Burdock, the grizzled security guard, towered over her. He was burly; he'd probably played football in high school, or maybe he'd been a wrestler, but that had been three decades ago. Now he just looked big and soft and a little messy. One of his shirttails had pulled free of his trousers. Still, a man of his size, soft and messy or not, could put a scare into almost anyone.

"You're early," she said as her heartbeat steadied.

"Mr. Bishop's orders. Sorry about what happened this morning. Don't know nothing about it."

"So Nath—Mr. Bishop told me."

Harry's faded blue eyes looked rheumy, as if he were a heavy drinker. Annie caught a whiff of whiskey on him. Could that be why he hadn't caught the vandal? Hopefully, he'd been warned.

"Good to see you, Mr. Burdock."

"Night, miss." He grinned at her. "Stay safe."

Was she imagining the tenor of that grin? To Annie, it appeared lascivious, and the way his gaze swept over her, she almost felt exposed. Unease followed her all the way to the corner, where she stopped and glanced back.

But Burdock was gone.

The café was still open. Coffee to go or not? *Not.* She didn't need another round of questioning from her friends. And John Riley was just inside the door, probably looking for an opportunity to chat up Helen. Besides, Annie didn't want caffeine keeping her awake, she decided, as the gallery owner glanced up and caught her looking in. She could use a good night's sleep.

So off she hurried across the street, still with that sense of being observed crawling up her spine. Busy glancing back over her shoulder, she didn't pay the traffic proper mind. A blared horn almost drove her out of her skin, and she skirted a turning SUV, the driver giving her the finger.

Lucky for her the curb was only steps away. She turned once more—no one following her, she noted—then went on her way.

Her imagination. Of course it was.

Suddenly, a familiar angry buzz cut through her thoughts. She'd barely made it a quarter of the way down the block when the motorcycle pulled up behind her.

Stumbling, she whipped around to see Nate pull his Harley to the curb, stop and remove his helmet.

"Going my way?" he asked.

The sound of his voice—that same seductive voice she'd heard in her head, the fantasy voice that had convinced her to unbutton her blouse—thrilled Annie down to her toes.

"Nate. What are you doing here?"

The same question she'd asked Nathaniel, but had expressed in a very different manner.

Nate unhooked a second helmet from his cycle—not a bike helmet, but a real motorcycle helmet—and held it out to her.

"Where did you get that?"

"I bought it for you."

"For me? You're serious?"

"So I could keep you safe."

Annie couldn't help herself. She couldn't help it that her pulse thrummed. She couldn't stop the warmth from spreading through her. And though the rational part of her tried to fight it, the other part, the primal part, didn't want to fight. It wanted her to indulge herself.

In Nate.

"Put it on, Annie." His soft demand was seductive. "Put it on and come fly with me."

Annie looked for an excuse not to, but her brain wouldn't cooperate. And neither would her body. As if she were mesmerized, she reached out, took the helmet and placed it on her head.

Nate stepped closer and fastened the strap. She held her breath as his fingers brushed the soft flesh under her chin and along her neck. Their effect rippled downward between her breasts, then spiraled out so that her nipples tightened into hard buds.

She choked out, "Where are we going?"

"Where do you want to go?"

Anywhere with you.

Before she could think of an intelligent reply—anything to not betray the sudden hunger that ran through her—Nate asked, "Hungry?"

Annie nearly choked. "Excuse me?"

Could the man read her mind?

"Hungry...for food?"

The way he said it convinced her that he knew exactly what she'd been thinking.

"Starving," she said.

True enough. She'd been running on adrenaline all day, and now her stomach was beginning to protest.

"Then let's eat."

Nate climbed back on the Harley, and when she

hesitated, he grabbed her wrist and swung her into position behind him.

Settling in back of Nate seemed so natural, as if she'd done it a thousand times, Annie thought. As if she belonged there. Belonged to him.

He headed northwest on Milwaukee Avenue. The ride grew longer than she'd expected, and she realized they were nearly to the suburbs before he finally pulled into an old-fashioned drive-in with individual speakers for each vehicle. They both dismounted to stretch, and he placed their orders—Polish sausage with everything, fries, onion rings and chocolate malts to go.

Leaning back against the Harley, she asked, "How do you know I wouldn't prefer vanilla?"

Nate's eyes narrowed as he loomed over her. "Not sinful enough." He placed one hand on either side of her and left only a hairsbreadth between them. "Unless I've read you wrong, you're a chocolate malt kind of girl."

Breathlessly, she murmured, "Okay, so you nailed me."

His grin had the effect of a stun gun. "Not yet. Give me time."

The strangled sound Annie made in return caused him to laugh out loud. As if it were the most natural thing in the world, she laughed with him.

"By the way, this place has the best Polish in the city," Nate said, pulling back and giving her some breathing room. "Trust me."

She did trust him, Annie realized. Totally and with abandon.

Otherwise, after the creepy feeling she'd had, why

had she gone off with Nate Bishop, a man she didn't know? She knew Nathaniel fairly well, but Nate was...well, a wild card.

Their food arrived and they headed out again. Five minutes later, they entered the local forest preserve.

"Um, I think I saw a sign that says this place is closed for the night," Annie said.

"It is. That's why I picked it. I want to be alone with you."

In a forest preserve? Annie swallowed hard.

Alone they were, in a small grove with a handful of picnic tables. She saw them just before he doused the headlights.

"It's, uh, majorly dark."

"Don't worry, your eyes will adjust."

They did a bit as he opened the saddlebags and rummaged around. A three-quarter moon hung cock-eyed in the star-filled sky and limned his every movement with silver. She stood still, her mouth watering at the smell of food as he set it on the nearest picnic table.

A match flared to life. Then a candle. Then two more candles.

He said, "I came prepared."

For anything? she wondered, his voice stirring her. And how prepared was she?

But maybe this was something she couldn't prepare for...attraction, liking, lust. Maybe she just needed to let go and trust that, this time, with this man, things would work out all right.

Nate grouped the candles in the middle of the picnic table, then straddled the bench on the side opposite where she stood.

"Sit," he said, ripping open the bags.

He didn't have to invite her twice. Mouth watering at the released smells, Annie clambered onto the bench. Nate slid her a Polish and a chocolate malt, then ripped open the fries and onion rings between them. Annie bit into her Polish and smacked her lips.

"So you approve?"

"You were right. This is the best."

"Would I offer you less?"

"Not so far," she admitted.

"I like a woman who appreciates her food."

"I like a man who appreciates a woman who appreciates her food."

"Then we're a match made in heaven."

Were they?

His image shimmered in the dark beyond the veil of candlelight. He appeared elusive, mysterious, sexy, with his hair falling over his forehead and shadowing his eyes.

Who was Nate Bishop? she wondered.

Beneath his leathers beat the heart of a man she wished she knew better. And maybe she would.

Hope spread through Annie for the first time in years as she stuffed herself silly. She was feeling silly in general. Eating drive-in food in a darkened forest preserve with a guy who rode a Harley made her feel silly and young and free.

And good. She couldn't ignore that she felt good about herself—better, in fact, than she had in years.

"So did you contact the exterminator?" Nate asked.

She stopped chewing long enough to echo, "The exterminator?"

"For the *rat!*"

He sounded a bit exasperated. And no wonder. Nate—*Nathaniel*—had given her the man's card, which she'd stuffed into a pocket.

"No, not yet. I didn't get a chance. Today was crazy," she said, remembering the exhaustive hours and the delayed closing. "We had more customers on a workday than we normally do on a weekend."

She saluted him with her malted and slurped some of the thick, cold chocolate through the straw.

"And the increase in customers would be due to...?"

"Word of what happened this morning must have spread like wildfire."

"Did they just stop and stare or did they shop for real and spend money?"

"Oh, they shopped, all right. If we did such great business every day I would be a happy woman."

"So money makes you happy?"

"Money doesn't make anyone happy. It just gives us the means to do what we were meant to do with our lives. It's how we use our lives that determines happiness."

"Then someone trashing your place—figuratively speaking, that is—didn't turn out to be all bad."

Earlier, she'd had a similar thought about any publicity being good publicity, and yet Nate's casually issued statement gave her pause.

Trying to shake the weird feeling she got from hearing his odd comment, Annie said, "There is no upside to someone's being purposely destructive."

"No, of course not."

She pierced the veil of golden light to look at him

more closely, but suddenly he seemed even more elusive. Like a stranger, in fact.

"I was just trying to put a positive spin on things." He cleared his throat. "I, uh, am a lawyer, after all."

Swallowing a mouthful of food, she nearly choked. "Lawyer? You?"

This was the first she'd heard of his being anything but a commercial landlord. Nate a lawyer... Somehow, the picture didn't fit. Nathaniel, maybe. But not her Nate!

"From a long line of lawyers, actually," he admitted. "The family firm specializes in real estate, hence my interest in commercial properties."

"So you practice law as well as own buildings?"

"Not anymore. With four commercial buildings to manage, and a few more on the horizon, I have enough on my plate to keep me busy."

So the apple really didn't fall far from the tree. Real estate law to real estate management wasn't much of a leap. Suddenly too full to take another bite, Annie set down the last of her Polish.

"I take it you don't approve?" he asked, his tone careful and very Nathanielesque.

"I'm just surprised."

"So was my family when I left the business to my father, uncle and cousin, and struck out on my own. What they were doing was fine for them, but for me...I just wanted something a little less dry, a little more inventive...with a little less structure and a lot more freedom," he explained.

Which made her feel better. Freedom she could understand. Now that she considered it, she really could see Nathaniel Bishop as a lawyer. But Nate was more freewheeling. Still, Nathaniel was her landlord....

Before she could dwell on the duality too deeply, he interrupted her thoughts. "So, does your family own a string of lingerie businesses?"

Annie snorted. "Hardly. Mom and Dad are both high school teachers in a conservative town in Indiana. Dad's the drama teacher and coach and Mom's an art teacher. She has always had her own studio, as well. She does some nice watercolors."

They were nice, Annie thought, if not her style.

"So that's where you get it."

"Get what?"

"The flare for drama and artistic sense, of course. You're the best of both of your parents."

She grinned. "At the moment they don't think so. They're pretty shocked by my choice of business, I can tell you. Mom thought I should open a store selling art supplies, and Dad thought I should have gotten a nice safe job with a megacompany that would appreciate my talents and protect me."

"But they didn't disown you."

"No, of course not. They love me. They just think I've made some poor choices with my life."

"That's got to be disappointing."

"Well, we can't have everyone's approval."

"You have mine," he murmured.

His voice went all low and throaty, sending little swirls of excitement along her nerves. She wished she were clever enough to counter with a witty comment, but she just couldn't come up with anything that didn't sound nerdy.

He asked, "So, do you have siblings? Are they like you?"

"Actually, I'm an only child."

"Ah, a true one-of-a-kind—I should have guessed."

He was actually making her blush. She could feel the heat rising along her collar and spreading into her cheeks. She could feel it lower, as well. A worm of sensual discomfort wiggled its way to her middle, crawled through her belly and took up residence in all the fine places she could name and some that she couldn't.

Just being with Nate made her feel special, and that was pretty scary stuff, because she didn't really know him. He wasn't at all like Nathaniel. She had known plenty of guys like her landlord and hadn't been better for the experience, either. But maybe with Nate she could take a chance.

So when he rounded the table and sat on the bench next to her, and it rocked with his added weight, she grabbed on to him. A reflex action.

They were facing in opposite directions. His back was to the candles, which left his face in darkness. Though she couldn't really see him, she could *feel* him. Sense him. And through that tenuous contact, she was caught.

"Annie..." he murmured, then slipped his right hand up to cup the side of her face. "I've been thinking about you all day. I've been thinking about doing this."

This was reaching up to undo her ponytail, letting her hair hang loose over her shoulders. *This* was following up the action with a kiss long enough and deep enough and sensual enough to peel off her socks.

They were barely touching except where their sides met and where he tangled his hand in the back of her hair and where his mouth assaulted hers, but she felt her entire being come alive. Not just her body, not just the outer shell, but what was inside her.

"I knew you would be like this."

"Like what?"

"Sweet...salty...luscious. Everything a man could desire."

He sounded as if he'd thought about this, had anticipated it, and Annie wondered where she'd been while his attraction for her had been developing.

The intensity of Nate's words were reflected in the kiss that followed. Hazy headed, Annie gave in to the moment and turned toward him so that their upper bodies pressed together. She couldn't get close enough, and when he ended the kiss and deliberately set her away from him, she experienced an odd sense of loss.

Something deep in the night forest scolded her, but she couldn't tell if it was bird or beast. And she didn't want to listen to any warnings. She just wanted more.

Moonlight outlined Nate's features as he stared into her face, as if he could read her in the near dark. He brushed her face with his fingertips and a thrill shot through her. She pressed her cheek into his hand. He cupped her face briefly before trailing his fingers lower.

A seductive breeze swept over them as he unzipped her jacket. The material fluttered like the wings of a butterfly as he worked it open very slowly, deliberately, as if waiting for her to object.

She didn't.

Taking a shaky breath, she inhaled the sweet scent of new-mown grass as he undid the top button of her shirt. Then another. The locks of hair he'd freed fluttered around her face. His fingers brushed upward, snatched a long strand and trailed it down her throat, down the valley between her breasts.

The sensations that assaulted her also froze her for a moment.

His mouth followed, teeth nipping at her throat, tongue trailing between sensitive mounds of flesh. His fingers found a peak through her silk bra, and his thumb flicked it into a hard nub. She gasped and moaned. When he kept up a pulsing assault on her nipple, her body arched toward him, seeking greater intimacy.

"You're mine, Annie," he murmured. "You know that, don't you?"

A haze of desire making her reckless, she almost agreed. She licked her lips, preparing to answer. But the words stuck in her throat.

Too fast, she thought. This was all too fast. She didn't even know Nate. Nathaniel, she knew—or at least she thought she did—but not Nate.

Besides, words might commit her. Might commit her body to his.

How beautiful that would be at this moment, she rationalized, in this place of glorious nature, his flesh in hers, stroking hot and wet, mating as the night whispered over their naked bodies.

Precautions—she had none with her. She wasn't physically prepared.

She wasn't mentally ready.

"Tell me you're mine," he urged again, his lips working their way back up to hers.

"No condom," she choked out instead.

"No problem. I have one."

But the spell was broken. Her thinking about it had ended the fantasy, at least for the moment. The fires still burned, but something more urgent intruded. Common sense.

She didn't know Nate, she reminded herself again. He hadn't told her much about himself except that he wanted more freedom, something more inventive than the life he'd had before. That might be enough to attract her, but not to reassure her.

"Please," she whispered as his mouth hovered over hers.

Groaning, he rolled away and thunked his back against the picnic table.

She glanced at him but, of course, couldn't see his face.

"I'm sorry."

"Don't be."

But as her hormones settled, her mood deflated, and she knew that she had made the right choice. If she'd had sex with Nate, she would feel even worse.

What was wrong with her? She'd nearly gotten herself into an untenable situation.

Again.

Everyone always said she was so sensible, so conservative—at least Nick and Helen thought so, when it came to men. She had thought so, too. But now, considering the things Nate stirred in her, she wasn't feeling conservative at all. She was feeling the way she had years ago, when she'd made such a horrible fool of herself.

Fear seared her insides. Not the kind she'd felt earlier, or the night before, but the kind that had stayed with her for nearly a decade—bad memories that went back to her early college days.

"Are you all right?"

"Of course," she lied. "I just don't usually take things so fast."

"Things?"

"Connections."

"You sound like you're making a telephone call."

"That sounds so...so impersonal."

"Exactly."

She gave him a stricken look. "I didn't mean to be insulting." Sensing his amusement, she asked, "Are you trying to provoke me?"

"If only I could."

Well, he'd succeeded in more ways than one, and she would bet that he knew it, too. He was making sport of something most men would get bent out of shape over.

But then he wasn't most men, or he would be on the offensive.

Before she could think of a way to smooth things over, he asked, "Ready to go?"

She wasn't ready. Not ready to leave him. But it was the smart thing to do, and he sounded resigned.

"Right. Rock has been alone all day. He's probably been watching for me since dusk."

"You think he knows that's when you're supposed to get home?"

"He's a smart cat. And his internal clock is sharper than ours. He'll be yelling about his dinner being late before I even get through the door."

"Then let's not keep him waiting any longer," Nate said, sliding off the bench. "We wouldn't want to get you in trouble with the male in your life."

Annie gave him a quick look, but of course she couldn't see his expression. Feeling weird—who wanted a pet to be the only male in her life?—she gathered up the discarded food wrappers, shoved them back in the paper bag and found the garbage can a few yards away. Nate doused the candle.

Then she was straddling the Harley again, pressed into Nate's back. The forced closeness wouldn't let her forget his touch or what she really wanted from him. Heat surrounded her all the way home.

But by the time Nate got her to her door, he seemed cool and collected, while she felt hot and frazzled. The wind in his face seemed to have worked wonders for him.

Annie fought the temptation to invite him in. Instead, she said, "Thanks for dinner and the ride home."

"You don't need me to check under your bed tonight?"

She needed to check *him* out *in* her bed—thoroughly—not that she was going to say so.

"I think I've got it covered," she croaked, taking a step back.

Before she could turn to unlock her door, Nate

swooped down on her, clenched her waist with an arm of steel and kissed her breathless.

Just as suddenly, he let her go, and she stood there, dazed, wondering what came next.

"I needed one for the road," he said softly. "Now get inside while the going is good."

Knees melting under her, she got the door open. Rock wasn't standing there waiting for her as expected. He sat by the bed, looking as if he were ready to disappear beneath it once more.

"Rock, honey, come here," she coaxed.

But the cat stayed where he was, meowing a complaint.

She turned for a last look at Nate, who'd already mounted up.

"Tomorrow," he said, before starting the engine.

And she couldn't tell if that was a promise or a threat.

5

"DO I HAVE TO SPELL it out for you?" asked a petulant voice. *"I...want...Annie!"*

Annie winced as she heard the demand ring out from the shop into her office, where she was downloading a couple of new orders from the Website.

"I'm sorry, Mr. Hardy," Gloria said, "but Ms. Wilder is busy."

"Too busy for a good customer?"

"It's not that, Mr. Hardy. You're one of our best customers. We've just had so much business in the past few days that she's behind with her paperwork."

"If paperwork is more important than a good customer..."

"Oh, no, never. But it would be my pleasure to—"

He cut her off. "I see I shall have to take my business elsewhere."

The statement popped Annie out of her chair and into the store, where the irritated man was glaring at her assistant manager. Normally he was a little pasty, but today he was red-faced, with the color spreading up into his thinning, pale blond hairline.

"Why, Mr. Hardy," she said as if she hadn't heard him, "how nice to see you, and so soon!"

Clive Hardy had taken up a full hour of her time barely a week before, and here he was again, no doubt ready to spend another several hundred dollars on her merchandise—but, it seemed, only if she waited on him personally. He'd been around a half-dozen times in the past two months. She was reluctant to lose such a customer even if he was a bit...well, eccentric, as she'd told Helen. Eccentric but harmless.

"What can I do for you today, Mr. Hardy?"

"Ah, there you are, Annie."

Her name vibrating from his too-thin lips and his pale gray eyes roaming over her made her shift away from him a bit. Harmless, she reminded herself. He wasn't much bigger than she was, anyway. Maybe he had a few inches and a few pounds on her, but she could handle him if he tried anything. Not that he would, of course. While he'd demanded her personal attention, he'd always remained a gentleman.

It was just that the uneasy climate recently—her thinking someone was following her, invading her home, was getting to her. And knowing that someone was trying to discredit her store.

She smiled and asked, "So what can I do for you today, Mr. Hardy?"

"I need something new and provocative for my Leslie."

Leslie being the name of his wife, assuming he actually had a woman at all. Gloria thought he had made up this Leslie's existence, and as proof had pointed to the fact that no wedding ring graced his hand. And Annie had pointed out that not every married man wore a wedding ring.

"Something provocative to wear?" Annie asked. "Or would you consider a scented massage oil? I just received a shipment of new products the other day."

His response, ''Something to wear,'' came as no surprise.

It was always the same. He made her pull out every new item—and lots of the old as well—and tried to decide if they would look good on *her*. Hardy insisted his Leslie was exactly Annie's size, had her exact coloring and her exact shade of hair. So she would be the perfect model if only she would try on the intimate apparel for him.

While she might be willing to wait on him on demand, Annie wasn't willing to go that far for a sale, not even a really big one.

''We have a whole new line of animal prints,'' she told him.

''Nighties?''

''And underwear.''

''Crotchless panties?'' he asked, licking his lips.

Annie fought the color rising to her cheeks. ''Of course.''

''Bras with holes to accent the pretty nipples?''

Annie blinked, and behind him Gloria was doing her best not to choke. He'd never been this frank before. Annie had never been totally comfortable with him, but today he was making her downright uneasy.

''I'm sure we have everything you want,'' she assured him.

Even if he *couldn't* have it all!

His oily smile when he said, ''Well, let us at them then,'' made her stomach queasy.

He bounded toward the back of the store where the naughtier apparel was displayed. After exchanging a look with Gloria, who indicated that she was willing to throw the man out bodily, Annie followed Hardy.

He was already fingering the crotchless zebra panties.

A strange light in his eyes, he asked, "Are you sure you wouldn't care to model these for me?"

Skin crawling, she said, "Positive."

The only man for whom she would consider modeling her merchandise was Nate Bishop.

Hardy sighed. "You must wear what you sell."

The question threw her. The letter from her secret admirer had asked the very same question. Surely *he* wasn't the one who'd sent it! She hadn't believed it when Helen had suggested as much, but maybe her friend had been right!

The thought depressed her, and Annie couldn't wait to be rid of Clive Hardy as he picked out every piece of see-through, zebra-striped lingerie he could find.

"Could you at least hold this up to yourself?" he said, holding out a nightie. "I just want to get an idea of what this will look like on my Leslie."

Hoping it would get rid of him faster, Annie held it up as requested. And then he gave her a second piece to hold up. And a third.

The sudden hunger in his eyes unsettled her, giving her second and third thoughts about what she was doing. And then, thankfully, just when she'd had enough, he retreated. Hardy was pushing it, getting bolder. The day when he walked into the store and she was alone...well, suffice it to say she would lose at least one big sale.

And big this one was. He bought several hundred dollars worth of lingerie, while Gloria's customer spent a more typical forty dollars. That meant Clive Hardy had racked up nearly a thousand dollars in Annie's Attic in the last month, she calculated as she counted out his change.

"Aren't you forgetting something?" he wheedled.

"What would that be?"

"Condoms." He indicated the display she'd set up the other day. "I understand you're giving freebies with each purchase. That means I get nine, right?"

"Yes, of course. Pick out whichever ones you like."

"You do it for me."

He wanted her to handpick condoms that he would use with his wife? Or whomever? *Ee-eow!* Compromising, she picked up an unopened box.

"Have a dozen, Mr. Hardy."

"This will do me for a night or two," he said with a sly smile, his gaze never leaving her face, as if he were looking for a reaction to this all-important information. "See you next week."

"Bye."

The moment he was out of the shop, Gloria said, "That man creeps me out!"

"He's not that bad," Annie insisted as usual, though she was rethinking her stance.

"The hell he ain't!"

"All right, so he was a little too suggestive this time."

"That man uses you in place of a real sex life. When he leaves here, he probably goes right into the alley to jerk off!"

"Gloria!"

But her assistant was wound up tight. "That pervert! Maybe I oughta send Julio after him. Julio *hates* perverts!"

"Leave Julio out of this!"

Gloria waved her finger at Annie. "You make life so difficult for yourself."

Right. Like getting involved with gang members would make her life easier.

Before they could argue about it further, the mailman entered the shop, followed by a couple of customers. Annie took the armful of mail and went back to the office, where she set it on her desk. It could wait. The influx of new customers couldn't.

While not as busy as the day before, they were kept hopping until two, at which time she insisted Gloria take a real lunch. Only a single customer came in during the next hour, so when Gloria returned, Annie left the shop to her and disappeared back into the office, where she was tempted to call Nate.

Not having heard from him all day, she missed him.

Bad, bad sign, she told herself, but the scolding wasn't convincing. No matter that she knew better than to get too deeply involved with a man. She couldn't help herself. Couldn't control her emotions.

Work. She needed to work to keep him from mind, so she finished filling the orders from the Website. Though small, the packages were stacking up. She really ought to get over to the post office.

She checked her watch. She had a half hour until commuters would descend from the rapid transit station. Again, not enough time to leave the shop, but plenty of time to check the mail delivered earlier. She sorted the stack on her desk into piles. Catalogues, bills, junk mail...and a familiar-looking envelope.

An envelope with no stamp, no postal markings. Just like the last time.

Her hand trembled as she stared at the innocent-looking envelope, wondering again who had sent it. Maybe this time the author had signed the missive. Only one way to find out.

She flicked open the seal and slipped out the single sheet of folded paper.

Dear Annie,

Do you like playing games? Of course you must. But what kind of games? Do you play out your own fantasies with men? Or do you prefer to rely on board games, the ones you sell in Annie's Attic?

I wonder if you play any kind of games when you're alone, and if you do...do you ever think of the man I could be for you?

An Admirer

Annie swallowed hard. There was more than one way to interpret the letter. Playing games. What had he meant by that? And who was *he?*

Clive Hardy immediately came to mind. He'd just been there, stirring up her doubts about him. Even if Helen's suggestion wasn't niggling her, Hardy would have come to mind after the way he'd acted earlier. And he'd left right before the mail had arrived. Could he have bribed the mailman to deliver something a little extra? Or perhaps he had just slipped the envelope into the carrier's bag when he'd been in another shop.

Of course, since the missive had been at the bottom

of the pile, the letter could have been on her desk already, and she simply hadn't noticed it until now. But then how had it gotten there? she wondered, even as Harry Burdock came to mind. With his set of master keys, the security guard had access to every business in the building.

She posed that theory later at the café after she'd closed up shop and her coffee-to-go had become a sit-down affair.

"Maybe you ought to call the police," Helen said.

"Police?" Nick echoed. "It's a letter from a secret admirer. Nothing threatening there."

"I'm telling you, it's that creep Clive Hardy. Don't let him in your shop again, Annie."

"He hasn't actually done anything to give me reason to keep him out."

"You're going to wait until something happens to you?" Helen demanded.

Which only made things worse. Rather than feeling better talking things over with her friends, Annie was finding that her nerves were on edge.

Wishing she had kept the letters to herself, she pleaded, "Can we change the subject?"

"Great. Let's talk about your love life. So spill."

From the frying pan into the flames. Was she a moron or what? Annie wondered.

"I have nothing to report."

"Excuse me?" Nick said with a grin. "You mean that wasn't you who got on the back of that motorcycle yesterday after work?"

"Why didn't you tell me?" Helen demanded.

"You might have run out there and tried to stop her."

"Oh, please!"

"You want to run everyone's life," Nick said, "so why pretend otherwise?"

"I just don't want Annie making a big mistake—"

"Uh, hello," Annie interrupted. "In case you two haven't noticed, I'm still sitting right here."

"Well, I'm serious," Helen said, turning her back on Nick. "This Clark Kent–Superman thing Nathaniel Bishop has going is just plain weird."

"You think everything is weird," Nick said. "You're suspicious of all men. Annie, ignore her. Go ahead and give the guy a chance. Everyone has parts of themselves they don't want to share with the world," he said.

Including herself. And Nick, too, Annie knew. There were dark parts that he kept to himself. Sometimes he got in a mood and did a disappearing act, only to show up a few days later as though he'd never been gone.

"You do have a good point."

"You bet I do. You're lucky Nathaniel is sharing himself up front with you."

Helen made a sound of exasperation. And Annie suspected she would have continued the argument, but John Riley strolled over from the counter, where he'd just gotten himself a coffee.

"Mind if I join you?"

Helen pulled out a chair for him, and Annie determined to bully her friend later into giving an update on her own sex life. She wanted *details!* Whatever Helen had going with Riley, she was keeping mum. That didn't mean Annie was about to let her off the hook.

"Listen, about Sunday," Annie said.

Helen gave her a blank look. "What about Sunday?"

"Don't play dumb. You're not old enough to have given up on birthdays yet."

"Yeah, I have two whole years before I hit the big thirty," Helen admitted. "When I was a kid I decided thirty was next to death. So next year I plan to celebrate my first twenty-ninth birthday, and the year after it'll be my second twenty-ninth birthday, and—"

Nick cut her off. "We get the idea."

"So what about Sunday?" Riley echoed.

And Annie saw her shot. "We're having an intimate birthday party for Helen at my place. Maybe you'd like to join us?"

"Intimate, you say? Count me in."

She would definitely have to get the goods from Helen. But that could wait. Rock couldn't.

"I'm off," she said as she stood.

"Before you go," Riley said, "I want to make sure that you're coming to my opening tomorrow night."

The next night being a first Friday, the traditional night for Chicago gallery openings.

"Me?" Annie arched her eyebrows in surprise.

"You weren't here yesterday or I would have checked with you then."

She looked at her friends. "So you two are going?"

"That's a definite maybe for me," Nick said. "But Helen's planning on it."

Annie just bet she was. "Then I'll probably stop by myself." If for no other reason than to see her friend operate on the gallery owner.

"Great." Riley saluted her with his coffee. "I'll count on your being there then."

Annie grabbed up her half-empty coffee cup. "See you guys tomorrow."

Nick smirked. "Don't take any rides from strangers."

Helen added, "Or from some two-faced man on a motorcycle."

Annie rolled her eyes and headed out the door.

Tonight Nate didn't catch up to her on the way home. Annie tried to sell herself on not being disappointed as she unlocked her front door, where Rock awaited her.

She roughed up the cat's fur, picked him up and kissed his pink nose. "I know you missed me, sweetheart."

He yowled in agreement.

"Okay, let's get you something to eat."

A few minutes later, he was chowing down and she was stripping off her clothes, when the telephone rang. Since she hadn't yet eaten, she let the answering machine pick up. No doubt it was a computer dialing with a salesperson ready to collar her if she dared answer.

"We're too busy to come to the phone right now, so leave a message at the beep." *Beep...*

"I was hoping you would be there."

She picked up the receiver. "It's you."

"You sound breathless."

"I just ran in the door," she lied.

Nate made her breathless. No matter that she knew this was going too fast, that she was too excited over a man she barely knew, he had the power to take her breath away.

"I miss you," he said. "I was hoping I'd get a chance to see you today."

"Why didn't you?"

"Work. And a little glitch in the family law business."

She gave a start. "I thought you didn't do that anymore."

"I don't, not usually. But there was a problem with one of my old clients, who happens to be in town checking on his properties. I needed to make nice to keep my family happy." Nate hesitated only a moment before saying, "So I was wondering if you could help me out."

"With what?"

"I need to attend a business dinner with my family members and the problem client Saturday night. It would be a lot more enjoyable if you would go with me."

A date? With Nathaniel? Annie couldn't help but be disappointed.

She'd been hoping for another date with Nate....

"I'm not really sure it's my kind of thing," she told him truthfully.

"It's not mine, either, but you know how family demands are."

Everyone had different family dynamics. Her parents would never pressure her into anything she didn't want to do, but she supposed if they tried she would cave.

"Well..."

"What can I say to convince you?"

"Give me something fun to look forward to."

"How about tomorrow night?"

"Gallery night," she said. "I'm sure you've noticed Gallery R across the street. We were personally invited by the owner."

His tone changing subtly, Nate echoed, "We?"

"Helen and Nick and me, though I'm not so sure Nick is planning on showing. And I think Helen's got something going on with Riley, or maybe it's just the flirtation stage, so I want to be there for backup."

"So *you* don't have a date?"

"No, no date."

"I'll make you a deal," he said. "I'll come with you to the art gallery opening tomorrow night if you'll come with me to dinner on Saturday."

"Deal," Annie said simply, her toes curling at the thought of going out with Nate so soon. "So what should I wear on Saturday?"

"I haven't seen all your merchandise, but I think I noticed something with tiger stripes."

The thought of his knowing what underwear she might choose made Annie squirm.

"I meant the outer garments," she said breathlessly. "Suit or dress?"

"I wouldn't mind seeing you in something soft and flowing."

"Got it."

"You certainly do. Wear whatever you want on the outside. Now, about that underwear..."

His tone was teasing, and he let his words drift off so that she could make of them what she chose.

She couldn't help herself. "So you like the tiger print."

"I would probably like anything on you. What are you wearing now?"

"Um, jeans and a T-shirt," she fibbed, never having had the chance to put them on.

"And under them?"

Annie swallowed hard. Did she want to play this game? The warmth curling in her stomach was hard to ignore.

"Serviceable cotton," she fibbed again.

"I don't believe you. I'll bet it's silk."

"Okay."

"What color?"

"White."

"Nope."

"Red?"

"Something more subtle," he insisted.

"Okay, peach."

"Like your skin. Does it feel like skin?"

"Uh, dunno."

"Touch it and tell me."

She hesitated.

"C'mon, no biggie," Nate murmured. "I just want to know if it feels as nice as your skin."

His tone seduced her into complying. She quickly touched the silk, then removed her fingers as if she'd burned them.

"It's smoother," she said, keeping her voice even. "Cooler."

"Mmm, I wish I was there so I could feel for myself."

Annie almost asked him who said she'd let him, but the words never came. She would let him and she knew it. And so did Nate.

"Where would you do it?" she asked. "Touch me, I mean."

"Everywhere. Do it for me, Annie. Touch yourself."

"Um, once was enough."

But he ignored her objection and went on. "Run your hand down your belly and spread your thighs just a little. Touch yourself there."

Heat flooded her and a throbbing began *exactly* there. Her hand seemed to move on its own, and she couldn't hold back a shaky sound when her fingers touched the damp spot on her panties.

Turned on by the idea of what she was doing, Annie nevertheless stopped when the heat of embarrassment flooded her. "I can't. I can't do this."

"C'mon, Annie, don't get so upset," Nate said smoothly. "After all, it's only a game."

6

ONLY A GAME…

Those words echoed in Annie's head all night and all Friday when she wasn't busy with a customer. The second letter from her admirer had been all about playing games, so what was she supposed to think? And when she finally made it to the post office with the orders from the Website, she was tempted to ask to speak to her carrier and ask him if he knew anything about the letter.

But then what?

The letters had been more titillating than threatening, the reason she'd defended them to Helen.

It was the game thing that bothered her, she decided. Her trust had been tarnished long ago, after the way Alan Cooper had played with her head.

But Nate wasn't Alan. Nate could be trusted.

Once she settled that in her mind, her tension eased.

No matter how much time had gone by, making those comparisons seemed impossible to stop. She felt absolutely Pavlovian sometimes, her reflex actions never letting up. Annie wished she could just get over the past, as Nick and Helen kept urging her to do.

She decided she wouldn't give either of them ammunition against Nate by telling them about her suspicions. After all, she didn't know for certain if Nate had written those letters. So discretion was called for when Helen arrived at the shop to meet her for the gallery opening. Annie didn't need her already disapproving friend on her case double-time.

As usual, Helen was in style, in magenta-silk cropped pants with little tassels at the calves and a cropped, salmon-silk top with even more tassels that kissed her flesh when she moved. Her feet were encased in backless pink-and-orange sandals with bizarrely shaped heels. And her hair was up in some kind of exotic do, with little fountains of blond curls that jiggled when she walked.

Feeling dowdy by comparison, Annie locked the shop door and headed back to the dressing room, where she'd changed clothes and put on a bit of makeup.

"I'll be ready as soon as I can figure out what to do with this hair."

"You're wearing a dress!" Helen said, as if suddenly noticing.

Annie looked down at the simple gray wraparound garment with flowing skirts, a throwback to her college days, but one that she'd hoped still looked in style. "Retarded, right?"

"No, I'm just surprised," Helen said, following her into the dressing room.

Cream-colored with pale pink accents wasn't her style, either, Annie thought, but she had to admit that the dressing room held the aura of romance, especially the plush chairs and the settee upholstered in soft rose shot with gold. Her customers loved it—one had jokingly threatened to move her bed in.

Helen said, "I haven't seen you so fancied up since... Hey, wait a minute, are you wearing that dress to impress Nathaniel?"

"No, of course not."

"You expect him to be there, don't you?"

"Not Nathaniel, no."

Annie glanced at herself in the mirror and wondered if she'd made a mistake with the gray dress, after all. The makeup looked pretty good though, despite her having to wear glasses to see. The reflection in the mirror gave her pause. Behind her, Helen had crossed her arms over her chest and was glaring at her.

"Okay, so you're looking forward to seeing Nate, then, right?"

"Mmm-hmm." Annie tried to act casual. "He'll be here in—" she checked her watch "—fifteen minutes."

"What? You actually made another date with him?"

"A *first* date."

His chasing a rodent and setting up a picnic in the forest preserve on the way home didn't count.

"Don't split hairs."

"Helen!" Annie faced her and pleaded, "Before you say anything else negative, know that I like Nate, okay? No, that's not exactly true. I *like* Nathaniel. But Nate...well, Nate is..."

"Dangerous?" Helen asked, before Annie could come up with a better word like *gorgeous* or *exciting* or *hot.*

"Why dangerous? Because he rides a motorcycle?"

"Because he's playing games with you."

Though she was certain Helen couldn't have made the same connection that she herself had, Annie shifted uneasily. "You don't know any such thing!"

But *she* did. *Only a game*... He'd said so.

"Okay, I'll reserve judgment," Helen agreed. "For the evening, anyway."

"Thank you. Now, about my hair..."

"Just sit and let me at it."

Annie wanted something softer than normal, but not too radical. Helen worked wonders with hair, but she had a whole different style, one that suited her bombshell looks. So Annie couldn't help being nervous, seeing that glint in her friend's eyes. But as always, Helen came through for her, making a loose French braid on one side, leaving a fall of rippling strands over one shoulder. Then she wound some silver ribbon from the shop around the rubber band to hide it, and wove the long tails through the loose hair.

Annie smiled when Helen let her look in the mirror. "I approve."

"Me, too," said a male voice behind them.

Heart racing, Annie turned to see Nate leaning against the doorjamb. No leathers on him tonight. Instead, he wore a deep blue shirt open at the throat and a pair of casual khaki pants and loafers.

All thoughts of game playing and danger flew from her mind, replaced by old-fashioned lust.

NATE WAS STARING appreciatively at Annie and at the dress he hoped she'd worn for him when Helen said, "Nathaniel, what a surprise."

He turned to the café owner. "Annie didn't tell you that I was joining you?"

"Oh, she told me, all right. But she also locked the front door, and yet here you are."

"I knocked on the window, but I guess you couldn't hear me in here."

"So you just used your passkey?"

"Actually, I came in through the back door." He looked beyond Helen to Annie. "I figured I might get your attention if I knocked there, but it was already open."

"The back door was open?" Annie said. "I could have sworn I locked that one, too."

"You obviously weren't in your right mind," Helen said. "You haven't been for days." She gave Nate a piercing look before she brushed by him.

He couldn't miss the disapproval in her stiff posture. What was Helen's problem with him?

"She's overprotective," Annie whispered, now close enough that he was affected by her light floral scent. "But she'll loosen up around you once she gets to know you."

What the hell was that supposed to mean? Helen did know him, if not as well as Annie. He'd been her landlord for months now.

Surely she didn't suspect…

Nate prepared himself for anything, but Helen didn't even speak to him as they left Annie's Attic and set off across the street, where Gallery R was bursting with people—more wine drinkers than patrons, he figured.

A half hour later, he and Annie sipped at their own glasses of wine while strolling into the back room of the gallery. Helen had done a disappearing act within minutes of their arrival, but now Nate saw that she was talking to John Riley.

The gallery owner looked up and saw them. Though Helen kept talking, Riley seemed to lose focus on whatever she was saying. His expression seemed…almost hostile. Had Helen been badmouthing him? Nate wondered.

Irritated, he turned to a wall of framed photographs and raised his eyebrows in appreciative surprise. "Hmm, this is some good work."

Annie glanced at the photographs, the subjects of which were women in various stages of undress.

"You can get more bang for your buck with a *Playboy,*" she commented. "I understand they have good articles, too."

Nate immediately swept Annie away from what he feared she would see as competition. He'd made a mistake on the phone with her. After she'd gotten so weird around him the day before, he didn't want any more negative thoughts entering her head where he was concerned.

And so approaching Helen and Riley was a big mistake.

"You've got a great crowd," Annie told the gallery owner.

"Yeah, I'm pleased," the man agreed. "Now if only the sales will match the turnout."

"How about you, big spender?" Helen asked, and Nate realized she was talking to him. "Don't you need some artwork for your office? Oops, sorry, that's not you, is it? That's Nathaniel Bishop, our landlord." Her tone was just short of snide.

Nate simply stared. He couldn't figure out why Helen was suddenly so hostile to him.

Not unless Nick had let something slip....

Surely not. Helen wasn't the type of woman who would keep that kind of information to herself. She would feel obliged to tell Annie everything she knew. And then it would be all over; he'd known that going in.

"Excuse us, I could use some air," Nate said, placing an arm around Annie's waist and leading her back the way they'd come.

"Where are we going?"

"For a walk."

"But the opening... Helen..."

"I think Helen's doing all right for herself," Nate said through clenched teeth. He stopped dead in his tracks. "But if staying is important to you, of course we can."

Annie looked back to where her friend was still talking to the gallery owner. And Riley was again staring in their direction, Nate noticed. He tried not to show how anxious he was to get out of there, while Annie made up her mind.

"What the heck," she finally said. "We made our appearance. Let's get out of here."

Once they were out of the gallery, Nate glanced over at her display window across the street. Annie had changed the display so that the female mannequin was now stepping out of her trousers, revealing a red satin thong bottom.

Thinking about seeing Annie in one of those got him hard in an instant. Was she wearing one? he wondered.

Maybe tonight he would find out.

"I DIDN'T REALIZE you lived so close by," Annie said as they walked north on Damen Avenue. When Nate had suggested they stop by his place, she'd hardly hesitated before agreeing.

"My commercial properties are nearby, so living here made sense," he said. "Besides, I like the neighborhood. You know, the local color can be pretty entertaining."

Indeed, on this lovely spring night the streets teemed with people, mostly in their twenties and early thirties. In addition to the more conservative crowd, there were the dyed and the tattooed and the pierced.

"I think we have more body piercings per square block than in any other neighborhood in the city," she said, spotting a couple that had all three eye-catching attributes.

Though the night air had cooled greatly, dozens of customers anticipating summer packed the local restaurants, while others crowded around little sidewalk tables outside of the many small cafés that lined the street. Personally, Annie was glad for Nate's arm around her, adding extra warmth.

At the end of the block, they turned onto a side street with historic "sunken" buildings. Annie knew that at one time the streets had been raised, and what had once been first floors in houses and apartment buildings had literally gone underground.

Nate's building was one of those. Constructed of brown brick, it had some nice touches she could see by streetlight—decorative tiles and stained-glass inserts in windows.

"Did you renovate the building yourself?" she

asked, as they walked up to what now was the first-floor porch.

"I have to admit I bought the building in really good shape. It already had new kitchens and baths, and redone hardwood floors. I just added a few touches of my own."

Inside the vestibule, he opened another door and they climbed another set of stairs.

"You like living high," she mused.

"I sort of duplexed my apartment."

Nathaniel, all Nathaniel, she thought, as they swept through a living area that was all beige and cream and caramel. She barely got a glimpse of the place before he led her up yet another staircase, to a door that didn't look original to the building.

Then he opened the door and the cool night air flowed over her.

"The roof?"

He led her outside, beneath a pergola entwined with blooming vines that smelled heavenly, and then out into the open. The rooftop was pure Nate, she noted with satisfaction.

Trees in planters. And flowers, lots of flowers. Some spilled from traditional containers, but most peeked from more fanciful objects—an old washtub, packing crates, even an old-fashioned pedestal sink.

"From commercial buildings I've renovated," he told her. "I hate waste."

"It's wonderful. How often do you use it?" she asked, checking out the lawn furniture, including a swing for two, a hammock and a small table and chairs tucked under the pergola.

"Not often enough, but once in awhile, especially at night. Sometimes I sleep out here."

He turned her by the shoulders so that she was facing southeast, and walked her over to the railing, a sturdy steel affair that would keep them from tumbling off the building. The view was incredible. The downtown skyline sparkled against the night sky, the skyscraper lights competing with the brilliant stars overhead.

"Such a clear night. So beautiful." Still she couldn't keep from shivering.

"Something wrong?"

"Just a little chilled," she said, and it wasn't entirely a fib.

"I can fix that."

Of course he could. He wrapped his arms around her. But his body heat didn't melt away the doubts that intruded uninvited—doubts that Helen had brought up. No, Annie couldn't put all the blame on her friend. She'd been fighting doubts since the night before....

But those doubts began melting away as Nate held her protectively, his head against hers, his warm breath laving her ear. Looking out over the city spread before them, Annie felt as if they were standing together at the edge of the world. Her stomach took a tumble—she'd never liked heights—but she fought the sensation.

She leaned back into Nate, rested her head against his shoulder, which fully exposed her throat. He took immediate advantage, lightly running his hand along its curve, dusting it with his warmth. Not the only place affected, she realized, as warmth curled through her stomach and spread a light glow of tension along her nerves.

Annie sighed. "That's nice."

"Is it?"

"Mmm."

"What else is nice?"

"You."

"I wasn't fishing for a compliment," Nate murmured in her ear. "I meant what else would *feel* nice?"

Remembering the phone conversation in which he'd nearly seduced her, she cautiously murmured, "Everything."

"That's a pretty big order. Can we start small?"

Laughing, she tried to turn in his arms for a kiss—that was a start, right?—but he held her fast, face forward against the railing.

"Nate, let me go."

"I don't think so." His voice roughened. "You don't want me to."

Annie tried to turn again, with no success. "How do you know what I want?"

"I'm psychic. I can read you, Annie Wilder. I can fulfill your wildest fantasies."

Her pulse suddenly rushing through her at his statement, she murmured, "Then why are you asking me what I want when you should know?"

"Trying to be polite...but maybe you don't want polite. Is that it?"

She experienced a moment's unease. Surely he wouldn't try to force her to do something that she didn't want to do.

But this was Nate, she reminded herself, the man

who had twice stopped himself the moment she'd indicated that she'd had enough.

"So what do you want, Annie?" Nate asked. "This?"

He slid his hands up the front of her dress, then cupped her breasts. Sensation spiraled through her.

"Yes. Oh, yes."

She rocked back into him, felt him hard against her buttocks.

"Tell me, Annie. Tell me what you want."

He was doing it to her again, trying to get her to talk like he had on the phone. "More," she mumbled.

"More what? More of the same? More variety?"

"Yes."

He squeezed her breasts gently and she thought she might faint. But he held her fast while his hands worked their way down to her waist. Sensations shot through her and multiplied, and when his fingers found the tie at her waist that had been keeping her dress together, she started.

Did he mean to remove her dress here, in public?

Then again, a rooftop garden in the dark wasn't exactly the same as the middle of a busy street, even if there were people coming and going below. Even if they looked up. She doubted they could see much.

"If you want me to stop, say so, Annie," he whispered in her ear.

She should tell him to stop. She should. But her body had other demands. She shook her head instead.

He tugged at the tie, and it came loose and the dress opened slightly. The cool spring air nipped at her exposed nipples. She hadn't been able to resist—she'd worn one of the bras she sold, that pretty tiger print he'd requested. The thin silk material covered all but the very tips of her breasts.

Why had she worn the tiger set tonight if not for this? she asked herself.

And then she lost rational thought as Nate caught both breasts in his hands again, this time finding the openings. She could feel his erection grow along her buttocks—to mammoth proportions, it seemed.

Her nipples were already hard buds. Sensitive hard buds. So when he thumbed them in a steady rhythm, she felt her knees grow weak. But with Nate's body pressing her into the rail, she was going nowhere.

"What is it you like?" he demanded, his voice whispering through the fine hairs around her ear. When she didn't answer, couldn't answer, words sticking in her throat, he murmured, "Do you like the idea of my doing you right here with people down on the street not having a clue?"

His *doing her?*

She squirmed at the unromantic choice of words.

But when he lightly flicked her nipples, she moaned and ignored the feeling of objection.

"You like this?" he asked, spreading a hand flat between her breasts and letting it descend to her belly and even lower. "Do you want me to touch you there?"

She suddenly grew restless, her hips rocking in answer. If she had thought she was turned on the night before, when they were on the telephone, she didn't have words to describe what he was making her feel now.

His fingers slid slowly over her panties, to find the

slit in the material. The moment he touched her, he groaned, "My God, you're wet. Is that for me?"

Annie had never talked frankly with a man before, so instead she murmured a sound of agreement.

"What do you like?" he asked, plunging a finger between her wet folds. "Talk to me, Annie. I need to know what you want me to do to you."

The moment he touched her clitoris, she choked out, "That!"

Sliding his finger across the sensitive flesh in a way that made her writhe, he went deeper, first with one finger, then, gradually, with two, never losing contact with the sexual trigger.

"Relax. Open up to me. If you fight it, you won't be able to feel it."

She wasn't fighting, Annie thought hazily. She was just trying to hang on. Trying not to fall. Her fingers curled around the rail for extra support as he probed deeper, silently demanding that she open for him.

She adjusted her stance slightly and felt a trickle of moisture against her inner thigh.

"That's it."

Nate leaned harder against her and easily plunged his fingers along the wet path. Annie rocked against his hand—how could she not? How could she resist the rhythm he started, slow and easy and shallow? And he was teasing her nipples hard with his free hand. One. The other. Then both.

Annie couldn't have stopped if she had wanted to. Nothing had ever driven her to the edge of desperation before now. Nothing but this. But him.

The intensity of sensation multiplied, yet the pinnacle remained elusive. She sobbed with wanting and still she couldn't reach it.

"Go for it, Annie," Nate urged, changing the rhythm. Deeper. Harder. Faster.

He had her. Front, back, top, bottom… She was his, just as he'd proclaimed.

"Please," she begged, as his fingers plunging in and out of her grew wetter, the sounds louder.

"Please what?" Nate whispered, kissing her neck.

Wanting the exquisite torture to peak, she bit her lip and moaned again.

He moaned, too, and suddenly she felt his mouth on the side of her neck, sucking, biting…

"Aah!"

The hint of pain sent her whirling over that safe edge. She was tumbling, headfirst, into the abyss.

7

NATE HUNG ON TO ANNIE, forcing himself to do no more than hold her. No matter that he had a hard-on the size of the Sears Tower, he wasn't going to do anything about it, not yet, not tonight, he reminded himself.

Tonight was for her, so that he could win her trust.

"Are you all right?" he asked.

"All right is an understatement." She turned in his arms. "What about you?"

"I'm great," he lied.

He doubted that he could walk at the moment. And with her pressed against his chest…

Annie was looking up at him, wide-eyed. As if she'd just discovered the best thing since sliced bread. He brushed her cheek and enjoyed the shaky little breath she took.

What an innocent.

Bewitched by her, Nate couldn't stop himself from kissing Annie. She slid her arms around his neck and her tongue into his mouth. Pliant against him, she felt boneless. His pulse began to pound. He'd never wanted any other woman with this intensity.

He'd thought he couldn't get harder, but this was becoming painful. Not only his physical state, but the knowledge that he wasn't planning on doing a damn thing about it. Not tonight. First he wanted her to be as intrigued with him as he was with her. To end the torture, he put her from him, the foot of space providing him with blessed relief.

He straightened her glasses, then began pulling her dress together.

"What are you doing?" she asked breathlessly.

"I figure you don't want to stay exposed."

"But what about you?"

"What about me?"

"Don't you want to..." She looked over to the hammock, then back at him, her expression incredulous. "I mean, you didn't exactly..."

"Didn't what?" he asked, as he fastened the front of her dress.

She licked her lips. "Didn't...get any...satisfaction."

"Who said I didn't?" he said softly, leading her back under the pergola, where he sat on a cushioned swing and pulled her down next to him. Wrapping his arm around her, he steeled himself against the urge to take her more conventionally, as she seemed so agreeable to doing. "As a matter of fact, I'm more satisfied than you can imagine."

She dropped her gaze to his erection. Or rather, where she guessed it to be. While he could see her face well enough to make out each beautiful feature, the light was negligible and he was wearing dark pants.

"Uh, you're sure?" she asked, making Nate smile.

All in good time, Annie, all in good time.

She wanted more. Good. He would keep her wanting, at least for now. And he would enjoy every moment of the wait. How innocent she really was. A more experienced woman wouldn't ask—she would just seduce him. Annie didn't seem to know how. Truth be told, that touched him, made what they had just shared more satisfying.

"Trust me," he murmured, pulling her close so that her head rested in the crook of his shoulder.

He stroked her hair, kissed her forehead, rubbed her arm when she shivered against him.

He hadn't been so satisfied in years.

THE STAR-STUDDED SKY, the heavy scent of flowers and the warm arm surrounding her relaxed Annie into dozing a little on Nate's shoulder.

Once awake, however, she couldn't help but feel a little weird around him, undoubtedly because the sex had been so one-sided. So as soon as he suggested he get her home, she readily agreed.

"Would you mind taking a taxi?" he asked.

"Taxi?"

"My car is in the shop and you're not exactly dressed for the Harley."

Annie almost suggested they walk, then realized that would keep them together a little too long for her comfort. She needed to be alone to think.

"A taxi would be fine."

He casually draped an arm around her back as they walked to Damen Avenue, where he hailed a cab. He opened the door, helped her in and gave the taxi driver her address.

"You're not coming?" she asked, then bit her tongue.

"I can if you really want me to."

"No, that's all right. I just wondered."

"Good night, then."

He leaned over and gave her a chaste kiss.

"Night," she murmured.

"Should I pick you up at the shop or at home tomorrow night?"

"Tomorrow?"

"Dinner with the difficult client," he reminded her.

Trying to keep things straight in her presently fuzzy head, Annie frowned. "Oh, right. Pick me up at home."

"See you at eight."

No, he wouldn't, she thought. *Nathaniel* would be picking her up—for some very boring business dinner.

Nate handed the driver a twenty, about quadruple the fare, then closed the door and banged on the roof, a signal for the driver to take off. The taxi began to creep through the Friday night traffic.

Annie looked back through the rear window, but to her disappointment Nate wasn't watching after her. He was racing across the street to his apartment.

Putting the Nate-Nathaniel problem out of her mind, Annie tried to reconcile what had just happened on his rooftop. He'd been building up to it, certainly. The hot kiss down by the lake. Then another hotter, more intimate embrace in the forest preserve.

Having sex in public seemed to be a turn-on for Nate. Not that they'd actually had sex.

But *she'd* had sex, Annie thought, trying to ignore the insistent urges from below that demanded more. So what if Nate hadn't entered her in the traditional way? She'd experienced the greatest orgasm of her life.

Not that she'd had many to compare it to, or could remember details of something that had happened so long ago. Alan Cooper had been the only other man she'd actually been that intimate with. She'd been sex-shy since. Not that she hadn't tried to loosen up, but her self-protective instincts had been stronger than her sex drive.

Besides, she always had her fantasies. And she knew how to take care of herself.

But why hadn't Nate wanted to go further? she wondered. How could her orgasm possibly have satisfied him? What did he get out of it? Was he playing some kind of game with her? Was Helen right about him?

Uneasy, she shook away her doubts. They'd gotten carried away, but he was trying not to rush her.

That had to be it.

Wondering when she was going to see Nate again—as opposed to Nathaniel—Annie mused that, if he had come home with her, she could have invited him to her place on Sunday to help celebrate Helen's birthday.

Then again, she wasn't sure her friend would appreciate his presence. But that was because Helen didn't know Nate like she did. Annie had hoped for more togetherness at the opening tonight—she'd been certain Nate's natural charm would have worked wonders on her friend—but Helen hadn't seemed amenable, and pushing it might have alienated her further. If Annie continued to see Nate, however, Helen would have to learn to accept him.

"Can't see no address. Is this the place?" the grizzled old taxi driver asked, making Annie start.

She hadn't even realized they'd left the main drag, but here they were, stopped in front of her building.

"Yep, it's the right place."

"Kinda spooky out here, ain't it?" he asked in a voice that sent a shiver up her spine. "I mean, you don't have many neighbors on this here street and you live alone, right?"

"I have a roommate," she informed him as she opened the door.

Well, technically Rock didn't pay for half the mortgage—he didn't even keep down the rat population—but he did keep her company.

"The place is dark, so it looks like you're alone for the moment. Too many weird things goin' on around here lately, especially to nice young ladies. I'll wait until you're in the door."

"Thanks," she muttered.

Now he'd spooked her.

Exiting the taxi, she looked around more carefully than usual. Was that a movement in the shadows at the far end of her building?

The hair at the back of her neck stood up, and she stared for a moment when she realized someone really was there, seemingly up to no good. Some big guy. Had he been watching for her? Before she could be certain, the man hurried off in the other direction.

She stared after him as she moved to the door, but the dark cloaked him, and if he looked back, she couldn't tell.

Who the hell was he? she wondered. And did he

actually want something with her or was he just "casing the joint" because it appeared abandoned?

For some reason—the man's size, no doubt—Harry Burdock came to mind. But what reason would the security guard have for hanging around her home?

As usual, Rock was waiting for her in the entryway. He yowled his disapproval of her long absence as she fastened the dead bolt behind her. She picked up the little vagabond and took comfort in holding him close while peeking out the spy hole for several minutes.

Thankfully, no shadow crossed her stoop.

Annie took a shaky breath and let the cat down. Then she opened the mailbox from the inside and removed that day's stack.

Rock complained again, louder this time.

"All right, all right. Don't get your fur ruffled," she said, setting the mail on the table next to the door and turning to pick him up again.

But she'd been in too much of a hurry and had set the pile down carelessly, so that a large envelope slipped off the top. It hit the floor and bounced straight toward Rock.

The cat flew upward, hissing.

"My goodness, you're jumpy," Annie said, recognizing the knot in her own stomach as she reached for the envelope. "What's wrong, boy?" she asked, noting Rock's green eyes were fixed on the envelope and his nose was twitching as if he didn't care for its smell.

"What? It smells like a rat?" Annie asked, laughing nervously, then remembering she still hadn't called the exterminator. But she hadn't seen another rodent after Nate had blocked the hole in the wall, either.

Rock growled again, and curiosity about what he might be objecting to—something inside?—made her open the envelope.

The contents stole her breath.

Glossy photographs. *Of her!*

The pulse in her throat ticked at she stared at pictures of herself dressed only in her underwear. The same underwear she'd been wearing the night before.

When she got to the last shot, her stomach twisted into a knot and threatened to empty itself.

She closed her eyes for a moment, hoping the nauseating image would disappear. But when she opened her eyes again, the glossy photograph of her was still there, unchanged, in living color.

Annie Wilder the wanton, she thought, and stared numbly at the expression on her face and her probing fingers disappearing between her thighs.

"NO, IT WASN'T MAILED," Annie said, having told her friends about the photos when they all met for Saturday morning coffee at the cybercafé. "That was the spooky thing."

"*That* was spooky?" Helen asked. "The idea of someone coming right up to your windows to look inside…?" She shuddered. "How sick is that?"

"So what are you going to do about it?" Nick asked.

"Cover my windows, for starters."

The night before, she'd been too paralyzed to act. She'd shut off all her lights and had huddled on her bed, holding Rock and staring at the windows, wondering if even then someone was staring back.

"Talk about closing the barn door after the cow gets out."

Annie shot to her feet. "I don't need lectures, Helen. I could use a little support from my friends."

Helen also rose and quickly put her arms around Annie. "I'm sorry, honey. I'm just mad for you. You're the last person in the world who deserves to be stalked."

"Stalked?" Knees suddenly weak, Annie sat back down before she collapsed.

"What else would you call it when some jerk sends you anonymous X-rated notes and then hangs around your place until he can get some X-rated shots, too?"

Not that Annie had told them what, exactly, she'd been doing in that last shot, just that she'd been in her underwear. She'd also left out the detail about her being on the phone with Nate. Who knew what conclusions Helen would draw then?

"You don't know the photos and letters were sent by the same person," Nick was saying to Helen.

"Oh, please. Both were slipped into her mail. Annie, have you compared the handwriting?"

"Actually, the envelope with the photos wasn't even addressed," Annie said.

Nick gave Helen a superior expression. "See?"

"I see that you're being obtuse," Helen muttered, "both of you. So, Annie, other than covering your windows, what do you plan on doing about this?"

Annie shrugged. "What else can I do?"

"Call the police, for one."

"I don't know...."

"What? You're afraid of getting some pervert in trouble?"

"I'm afraid they won't take me seriously." And why should she open herself up to public scrutiny?

"Why not?"

"No threat. The letters weren't threatening and neither were the pictures. I'm not even sure they would be considered invasion of privacy. Don't you remember that case where some guy photographed a couple making love in the privacy of their own home through the windows, and then sold the photos? The guy got off scot-free."

"This is different."

"I don't see how," Annie insisted. "And how many stories have we heard about women who had men stalking them—calling them, following them—but because there were no actual threats to life or limb the police couldn't do anything? Just the other day, I saw a woman on television talking about how she'd even picked up and moved to a different city to get away from her stalker, but he always managed to find her, even when she changed her name. And the police never even arrested him because they said he never actually tried to *hurt* her, therefore they had no grounds." Even as she spoke, the sick feeling in her stomach intensified. "I don't even know for certain if I am being stalked, or if I am, by whom."

"If someone is stalking you, Annie, *I'll* do something to stop the bastard," Nick promised darkly, sending a shudder of apprehension through her.

"Like what?"

"Like get you some old-fashioned justice."

Annie didn't want to know the details. There was

a side of Nick that scared her sometimes. Not that she ever thought he would hurt *her.* But in addition to disappearing for days at a time, he never spoke about his past. What dark shadows lurked there? she wondered. For all she knew about his background, he might have been born on that first day of college when they'd met.

"I'd better get back to the shop," she said. "Thanks for listening."

Doing an about-face, Nick gave her a thumbs-up. "Hey, what are friends for, anyway?"

Not that it made Annie feel any better.

Stalked... How had that happened to her? Whose fantasies had she inspired? Other than Nate's...

Helen walked with her. "Want to catch a movie tonight?"

Annie forced away the negative thoughts. "Saturday night and you're free?"

"As a bird."

What in the world was the matter with John Riley? Annie wondered. Why didn't the gallery owner have Helen tied up for the night? Or was it Helen herself? While the café owner wasn't into hookups any more than she herself was, Helen certainly avoided long-term relationships with the numerous men who flitted in and out of her life.

"I wouldn't mind a movie," Annie said, "but I have this dinner I promised to attend."

Helen narrowed her gaze. "Nate again."

"No, Nathaniel. It's a business dinner. He'll be in his lawyer mode."

"Oh, Annie." Helen appeared to be in pain. "I'm really wondering about your judgment. So many things happening to you or your store in the past month and you not involving the police. Now this.''

This being her going out with either Nate or Nathaniel, Annie knew. ''I'll be fine.''

''I hope so. I would hate to see you get horribly fooled by a man who was no good for you. Again.''

''I'm a big girl, as you've been reminding me forever,'' Annie said. ''I have to take a chance sometime.'' Now that she had finally opened the door to a man, she wasn't ready to slam it in his face. ''I do have needs.''

''You're sleeping with him?''

''Not exactly. Not yet.''

Helen groaned, and Annie gave her a hug before hitting the street. She only wished her friend would chill out before doubting Nate became contagious.

When she got back to the shop, both Gloria and Chantal Williams, the part-time clerk who was a design student the rest of the week, had their hands full. Annie joined in and for a few hours forgot all about stalkers.

But when the crowd thinned and sales slowed, there it was again, in the back of her mind. All she could think about was covering up those windows.

''Do you two think you can handle the store alone for the rest of the day?''

''Hot date?'' Chantal asked, her thin, dark face showing her surprise.

Reminded of the dinner with Nathaniel, Annie muttered, ''Yeah, something like that.''

''Humph.'' Gloria crossed her arms and gave her a probing look. ''You don't sound properly enthusiastic.''

"I'm just tired," Annie replied.

Which was true, since she'd hardly slept at all the night before.

She left with her staff's blessings. All the way home, she toyed with the idea of canceling the dinner with Nathaniel, but then she'd be facing a night alone. Besides, she might start out the evening with Nathaniel and end it with Nate. Just the thought of Nate's hands on her again made her toes—and other, more vital places—curl with pleasure.

And who knew? If she stayed home alone, some pervert might be lurking outside, peeking in. Annie shuddered at the thought. Determined to fix that, the first thing she did upon arriving at home—after feeding Rock, of course—was to hit the upper floor and the room crammed with her estate sale treasures.

Rock followed, meowing in complaint.

"Gonna help me?" she asked the cat, opening a few boxes.

From one of them, she pulled out a gold tassel and dangled it before his nose. She grinned as he batted the thing with both paws. Letting him have the makeshift toy to carry around like a prize, she dug into one of the boxes filled with draperies and found exactly what she'd been looking for.

After dragging the heavy material down to her living space, she found a hammer and a box of nails. Having no window hardware, she improvised, draping and nailing. She would have all the privacy she needed, yet would still get plenty of light from the upper windows.

Several hours later, Annie looked around with satisfaction. All the windows with a line of sight to her living area were artfully covered with gold-shot cream cloth. In addition to improving the looks of her near barren living space, it made the lower windows impenetrable to anyone who didn't have X-ray vision.

X-ray vision…

The Superman reference reminded her of Nate, and of her date with Clark Kent. Checking the clock, she saw that it was after seven.

Just enough time to prepare herself for a date that would probably be as exciting as a funeral.

NATE WAS DISGRUNTLED that Annie wasn't wearing the same soft wrap dress that she'd had on the night before. All day he'd been imagining peeling it off her, this time to finish what he'd started.

Tonight, he'd thought. Tonight he would have her.

He'd fantasized taking her over and over again until she couldn't think straight. He'd never met anyone like her—at least not anyone he'd been attracted to. Normally he'd hooked up with flashy women with a lot of confidence. But he'd found the ones he'd dated to be empty inside. They wore everything they had on the outside, and when you looked past that…

Truth be told, Annie's display windows had intrigued him from the first. People said the eyes are the windows to the soul. But in this case, Annie's display windows told him all he needed to know about her.

But to his disappointment, tonight wasn't starting off the way he'd hoped. In addition to wearing a plain navy pantsuit and silk sweater, Annie just didn't seem to be herself. Subdued and a little distracted, she wasn't at all like the warm, passionate woman he'd experienced the night before. To top it off, he would swear she was purposely leaning away from him in the car.

"What restaurant are we going to?" she suddenly asked, as if just now realizing they were on the expressway heading north.

"No restaurant. My father's home. His and Chloe's now—that's his new wife."

"Oh."

Annie didn't sound thrilled. Nate could hardly blame her. For a girl who got off on a Harley and a Polish in the forest preserve, a ride in an Acura and a sedate dinner in Winnetka probably seemed tame by comparison.

"They're not that bad," he insisted.

She roused herself to give him a perfunctory smile. "I'm sure they're not."

"Did something happen today?" he asked, wondering where his Annie had gone. The woman in the car beside him was a dull imitation of the one who had fascinated him for months. "Any more attacks on the shop?"

"The shop's fine."

But she wasn't. Try as he might, Nate couldn't get her to talk about it. And though he had an idea of what might be bothering her, he certainly couldn't get into it or she would know.

The moment they stepped into his father's palatial home and crossed the marble floor to the cream-and-gilt living room Chloe had decorated, Annie shut down even more.

"Ah, Nathaniel, darling, there you are," his stepmother said, kissing the air next to his cheek. "You must introduce your little friend."

"Annie Wilder, meet Chloe Lamont Bishop. And this is my father, Eugene." He indicated the couple on the sofa. "Frank Mancuso and his lovely friend..."

Damn, he'd forgotten her name.

"Cookie," the buxom blonde piped up.

Annie managed a polite greeting, but for some reason seemed uncomfortable. Surely she wasn't intimidated.

As his father opened a bottle of Pinot Noir, he asked, "And what do you do, Annie?"

"I have my own business."

Nate added, "Annie rents one of my storefronts over at the six-corners building."

"Really," Chloe said. "You run the little coffee shop?"

"The lingerie shop. Annie's Attic."

"Really," Chloe murmured again. Her tone altered so slightly that Nate figured he and his father were the only ones to recognize her disapproval.

"I love sexy lingerie and so does my Frankie," Cookie stated.

"Got any hot new stuff we should know about?" Frank Mancuso asked. His hand heavy with gold rings, he squeezed the blonde. "My Cookie here looks good in anything...or nothing."

He laughed heartily, Cookie giggled, Eugene smiled and Chloe went very, very still.

And Annie looked as if she wanted to be a million miles away from the place.

Not that she said anything of the kind.

But Nate knew her well enough to know that she suffered through drinks. She suffered through dinner. She suffered another half hour of inane conversation with one of the law firm's richest clients—no questions asked about how he'd gotten so wealthy—and his dizzy if sweet Las Vegas showgirl companion.

The client and date were the reason Nate had been summoned in the first place; he wasn't as uptight as the rest of his family and could make any client, even a purported mobster, comfortable. Unlike his more conservative father, he'd never had a problem dealing with Frank Mancuso and whoever was on his arm for the evening. But tonight Nate was more worried about losing Annie than about some business that was a done deal whether or not he stuck around. So the moment he spotted an opening after they left the table, he made their excuses and whisked Annie out of there.

Pulling the car away from the house, he said, "Sorry you didn't have a better time."

Rather than responding to that directly, Annie murmured, "Unusual client."

"The only thing our law firm does for Mancuso concerns real estate, though he does have a reputation for certain kinds of unapproved activities," Nate admitted, not wanting to use the word *illegal.* "Chloe certainly doesn't approve of him. That's the reason I was summoned—to act as a buffer between him and Chloe."

"Your stepmother tried to hide it, but I could tell she didn't like him or his girlfriend." Annie hesitated only a beat before adding, "She didn't approve of me, either."

"I don't seek Chloe's approval about anything, certainly not about the women I date. She can be charming, but she's also a snob. My father has to live with her, but thankfully, I don't."

"Mmm."

A noncommittal response. Then again, Annie had been in a noncommittal mood since he'd picked her up.

This didn't bode well for him, Nate thought, gripping the steering wheel in disappointment.

No Annie in his arms. No Annie in his bed. He could hardly stand it.

Turning onto the expressway, knowing his plans for the rest of the night were already thwarted, and with no clue as to how he could salvage them, Nate sank into a dark mood of his own.

8

THEY WERE ALMOST BACK to her place before Nathaniel asked, ''So what happened today?''

Annie started. She'd been thinking about Mancuso, about his connection to a possible criminal. And that had somehow led her back to the photographs. And to her being alone again. Could Nathaniel read her mind?

She tried to thwart him. ''What makes you think something happened?''

''I'm not deaf, dumb and blind, Annie,'' he said tersely. ''Something's wrong. So what is it?''

Annie sighed. Of course she needed to tell him. After all, hadn't he come to her rescue the moment she'd called him the other night? Besides, in a roundabout way, he *was* involved in what the camera had captured.

''Someone left me some photographs,'' she said. ''In a big envelope, no postage, but stuck in with the regular mail.''

''At the shop?''

''At home.''

''So what's so upsetting about these photographs?''

''They're of me,'' Annie said, wondering why his voice had gone so tight. ''In my underwear.'' Before she lost her nerve, she went on quickly. ''They were shot the other night, when you and I were on the phone. They're a little, um...embarrassing,'' she said, in lieu of a better word that fully described her feeling of violation.

Though she noticed his hands tighten a bit on the steering wheel, Nathaniel didn't sound particularly shocked when he said, ''I knew you needed a security system.''

''What I needed was window coverings! Now I have them.''

Annie nearly bit her own tongue after snapping at him. He was only making suggestions in her best interests. But she did have a mind of her own, and everyone always seemed to know what she should do. Her parents. Helen. Now him.

As an only child, she'd been overprotected. And now that she was out on her own, she wanted to feel like an adult—difficult to do when everyone was always watching out for her. She didn't want to be left alone; she just wanted a support system, as opposed to another set of parents.

''So you have no idea of how the envelope got into your mail?'' Nathaniel asked.

''I thought I saw someone I knew when I got out of the taxi. Harry Burdock.''

''Burdock? Are you certain?''

''Not really,'' Annie admitted. ''The guy was too far away and it was dark. But he was big and his size reminded me of your security guard.'' Wondering whether she should say more, she decided to go for it. ''The other night Burdock gave me a scare...and I, uh, think he kind of liked it.''

Voice tight, Nathaniel said, "I'll have a talk with him," before withdrawing into a thoughtful silence.

Feeling better that she'd gotten all that off her chest, Annie stared out the window into the dark, wondering how she was going to handle the personal stuff that was to come once they arrived at her place. After the night before, he would no doubt assume that they would get down and dirty....

But this was Nathaniel. Straight-arrow Nathaniel. Not the guy she was having fantasies over.

By the time they pulled up in front of her place, Annie felt tense enough to explode, and determined to avoid a sexual confrontation. Not even waiting for him to round the car, she opened her door herself and jumped out.

"I'm really tired. Long day. Long, *hard* day," she stated as she inched her way toward her front door. "We had lots of customers. And the window coverings—did those, too, remember."

"You sound wired," he said, closing the car door behind her. "Maybe a glass of wine will mellow you out."

"No wine."

Though she kept inching away from him, Nathaniel moved in on her. Knowing he meant to kiss her—maybe more—Annie took a big step back.

"It's late," she said.

He hesitated, but only for a minute before asking, "Too late for a good-night kiss?"

Not knowing how exactly to get out of it without hurting his feelings, Annie licked her lips and murmured, "Well, if that's all..."

His expression was odd as he closed the gap between them. "Are you sure that's all you want?" he asked.

"Positive."

Still, when he kissed her, he put his all into it, Annie noted, immediately pulling away mentally. The kiss was pleasant but not earth-shattering. Not like Nate's kisses.

She pushed at his chest and stepped back, not knowing what to say. *We'll do it again sometime?* Well, maybe she would…with Nate. Not that she could tell Nathaniel that.

"I'm getting the feeling that I did something to offend you last night."

Staring up into his face, she noted the tightness tugging at his eyes and mouth, and something in her stirred in response. "I—I wasn't offended."

"You're sure?"

"Positive."

Though she was feeling more confused than anything, she merely said, "I'm a little freaked out over the photographs." Which, of course, was the truth.

"Maybe I should come in and take a look."

Her pulse jolted her as she thought of the conservative Nathaniel inspecting a photograph of her touching herself. "No, really. I'm tired. Some other time."

He stared down at her. Maybe it was the way the streetlights cast shadows across his face, but the man towering over her suddenly looked like a stranger to her. Like some guy she didn't know at all. Not Nathaniel. Not Nate. Uncertainty curled through her and she took another step away from him, backing straight into the door.

"You can't run from me, Annie," he said, stepping closer, flattening both hands on the jambs on either side of her. "Sooner or later you're going to come to terms with what you want from me. What I can give you..."

Her heart thundered as she said, "Now that's a little arrogant, don't you think?"

"Just stating the facts."

The fact was he was suddenly too close to her. A frisson of something undefinable slid up her spine. Something uncomfortable, edgy and yet somehow titillating....

Before she could think of what to do, he stepped back and she was face-to-face with Nathaniel again. Handsome, nice-guy, conservative Nathaniel.

"Good night, Annie."

"Night," she gasped, clasping together hands that suddenly trembled.

Remembering that she had to unlock her door, she did so with him looking on from a distance. He didn't drive off until she was safely inside...leaving her more confused.

Annie tried talking it over with Rock later, but he wasn't much help. He kept rolling over and giving her his tummy to scratch. At least she had a great relationship with the cat, she thought ironically, remembering the comment about Rock being the male in her life.

The phone startled them both. The cat jumped to his feet in a crouch, and Annie felt her pulse spike.

Hoping against hope that it was Nate—he'd had enough time to get home by now—she took a deep breath and picked up the receiver. "Hello."

No answer.

But she could tell there was a live connection, that someone was on the line.

"Hello!" she said more emphatically.

Then a chill set in at the sound of heavy breathing on the other end.

She wished she had caller ID so that she could get the number of the pervert who was trying to play with her mind. Then she would nail him....

"I take it you're not going to identify yourself, so I'm going to hang up now!" she said indignantly. "And don't bother calling me again!"

She hesitated a second too long. Long enough to hear the whispered, "You can't hide from me," in a rough male voice that she couldn't identify and that sent a chill up her spine.

After slamming down the receiver, she stared at it, her pulse pounding in her ears. Then she picked up the phone and punched in the code to reverse the call.

No dice. The pervert had obviously blocked his number. Wouldn't you know it.

No sooner had she hung up then the phone rang again. She picked up the receiver just high enough to slam it down in its cradle again. No way was she going to play this guy's game. And when the phone rang a third time, she simply disconnected the line.

Restless now, she had no urge to sleep. It was too early, anyway. To get her mind off her personal situation, she set it on work. On the store. On the *display window...*

Damn, she hadn't changed it. She'd been so anxious to get home to cover the eyes to her living space that she'd forgotten all about the store display.

You can't hide from me....

The whispered words echoed in her head, and she came to the conclusion that the caller and the photographer must be one and the same person. But what good would that knowledge do her?

She forced her thoughts back to Annie's Attic. People would expect to see a change in the display window, a little more heat between the fantasy couple. And she was going to give it to them.

No matter that it was after midnight. The thought plagued her until she knew she had to go back to the store and take care of it tonight. Otherwise she would have to get up at dawn, so that she could beat the early morning commuters who would pass her store windows. And sleep might be a precious commodity at the rate she was going. Now was the time.

Not that she was foolish enough to walk the streets this late at night. Instead she called for a taxi. By the time she changed into jeans and a T-shirt, it had arrived.

Ten minutes later, she was in her shop, moving around in the dark. Feeling safer, somehow—probably an illusion—she chose to leave the lights off, all but the low bulb in the window display, just enough illumination to see what she was doing.

You can't hide from me....

Staring out the plate glass, she saw only a few people on the street, no one remotely interested in her or her store. So she knelt down next to the board game and picked up the dice. As she did so, she couldn't help being struck by how much the male mannequin suddenly reminded her of Nate. And she couldn't help wondering if he would wear silk boxers covered with lipstick prints. She imagined he might not wear underwear at all.

That thought making her restless, she quickly rolled the dice and moved the pawn around the board. As fate would have it, the next article to be stripped from the display were those very boxers.

Weirdly, her hands trembled as she pulled them down the male mannequin's body. She couldn't help herself; she kept thinking of Nate, of doing this to him. Doing more. Touching him. Tasting him. Turning him on and making him come as he'd done to her the night before.

But then he would take the lead, because he was Nate. In control, if in a totally agreeable way. She couldn't resist him, couldn't deny him anything. Her head began to buzz pleasantly at the thought of letting him have his way with her wherever, whenever, whatever.

Her mind drifted back to that New Orleans fantasy....

She walked down the dark, exotic street, the scent of honeysuckle in the air. The trickle of water called her, and she followed its siren lure into a courtyard.

Dipping her hand into the fountain, she smoothed water along her arched neck.

"I'm just so terribly hot," she murmured.

"Then take off your dress," the seductive voice urged from the shadows.

This time, she couldn't undo the pearl buttons fast enough. Heat slicked her, and not only on the outside. Moisture gathered between her thighs as she heard him move toward her.

From behind, he touched her intimately as he removed her dress and tossed it to the ground.

"Now what?" he murmured.

She shrugged her naked shoulders. He stroked her lightly, just enough to make her hotter and wetter.

"Tell me what you want," he whispered.

"You know what I want," she insisted, arching her neck for him.

"So I do," he said, laving her ear, her neck, the soft place where it met her shoulder.

Now it was going to happen, she thought. Now he would turn her around and take her. Enter her. Dive deep into her until she was mindless with ecstasy. Then she would—

Her eyes widened when she felt the sharp prick like thin knives sinking into her flesh.

"What are you doing?" she gasped.

"Making you mine, Annie," he murmured as he feasted on her blood. "Making you mine for now and forever."

Annie came to from the fantasy with a start. Nate a vampire? What kind of trick was her mind playing on her now? A vampire was dangerous, the most dangerous kind of stalker possible.

Stop it! Nate is not dangerous!

Helen had twisted her mind with her negativity, her unfounded suspicions.

Annie rearranged the mannequin's body so that she could cover the area of sexual interest, draping the boxers over one hip. A real tease, she knew, but what else was she supposed to do? She hadn't actually thought out the display to the end. She'd merely played the game.

It's only a game....

Nate's words echoed through her head as, from the corner of her eye, she caught a movement in the shadows outside the window. Starting, she swung around, to see the silhouette of a man—so close that only the glass separated them.

Still on her knees, Annie fell to her butt and scooted away from the window, panic setting in until she recognized the familiar figure in black leathers. Even then she didn't relax, especially not when, with her eyes adjusting to the darkened figure, she swore a knowing smile tugged at Nate's sensual lips.

Unsettled and uncertain, Annie still couldn't stop herself from getting to her feet and going to the door. As if she were under his power, mesmerized, she couldn't resist. Then she realized how ridiculous that thought was.

This was Nate, she told herself. Nate. The man she wanted more than anything.

Unlocking the door and opening it, she murmured, "What are you doing here?" as he slid through.

"I was worried about you. I called—"

"You called?" Her pulse jacked up a beat.

"Twice. The first time I heard the phone slam back down. The second it just kept ringing and ringing."

Then he hadn't been the one who'd whispered so frighteningly to her, right? Maybe she should ask Nate directly, look for his reaction.

But before she could do so, he said, "I thought something was wrong—I mean, after your telling me about those photographs and all—so I rushed over to your place in time to see you getting into the taxi."

"You followed me?"

He shrugged and his smile didn't seem at all apologetic.

"Then you've been standing out there, watching me?" she asked. *Isn't that what a stalker would do?* a little voice out of nowhere asked. "For how long?"

"Long enough. Mmm, that expression on your face..." he murmured in a low tone that stole her breath. "I would have given anything to have been in your mind right then."

Not about to tell him that he had been, she said, "I forgot to change the display earlier."

"So you go out in the middle of the night."

"It was barely past midnight when I left home," she argued. "I was perfectly safe."

"Are you?"

A strange way of putting it, Annie thought. As if even now she shouldn't feel safe. Because of him? Her mouth went dry.

What was he trying to say? Was he warning her in a roundabout way? A frisson of something she didn't want to name slid up her spine.

He moved forward, the mere heat of his body pushing her back into the shop. Desire? Or fear?

"Um, actually, I was just getting ready to leave."

"Then get your things."

"Already have them." She patted one pocket. "Wallet." And pulled a handful of metal from the other. "Keys."

She started past him toward the door.

"Why do you take chances?" he asked softly, raising the hair at the back of her neck.

The fantasy of Nate as a vampire flashed through her mind. She turned and shifted away from him, trying to shake off the lethargic feeling from her limbs. She was not mesmerized!

"Life would be pretty dull if I didn't," she said flippantly, suddenly aware of that New Orleans-style dewiness covering her body. "I would be as smothered as if I were carefully wrapped up in cotton."

With that she opened the door and let Nate move past her, brushing her body, pebbling it with a flare of desire that threatened to take over her mind. Totally different from her earlier reaction to him—rather, to Nathaniel, she corrected herself, fighting the confusion that that duality caused her.

This was her fantasy and she could feel any way she wanted about anyone she wanted. No matter her doubts—and she was beginning to have a few—she certainly wanted Nate.

Locking the shop door, she tried to get her hormones under control, an impossible task with him standing so close behind her that she could feel his warm breath feathering the back of her head.

"Is that what your parents did to you as an only child?" he asked softly. "They smothered you?"

She started and nearly dropped the keys. "Let's leave my parents out of this."

Nothing like talk of family members, who would definitely disapprove of the chances she had been taking lately—Nate included—to deflate a good sexual buzz.

"Hmm, interesting."

She turned, but he was in the way and she couldn't pass him without rubbing against him. His heat pressed against her as he stared down at her, a predator to her prey.

But that wasn't her talking, that was Helen, Annie told herself. Nate was not a sexual predator. She'd invited him in, so to speak.

"How were you getting home?" he asked.

"The same way I got here."

"Can I seduce you into letting me give you a ride?"

Breathless at his choice of words, Annie was certain he could seduce her into nearly anything. Too far gone to object, she looked around. No Harley.

"Where's the bike?"

"Behind the building, in the alley." Leading her in that direction, Nate mused, "So where were we? Taking chances. Is that what turns you on?"

Was it? She didn't really know anymore.

Even so, Annie protested, "I, uh, didn't say that. Not exactly."

"You didn't have to. What would you say if I suggested we do something daring right now?"

She stopped dead in her tracks. "Now? How daring?"

"Name it."

"Me? This was *your* suggestion."

"So I have to come up with the risk," he mused, leading her toward the alley once more.

"An acceptable risk."

"Define acceptable."

"Daring, fun, but no one gets hurt."

"So danger doesn't turn you on?"

Danger? Whoa! Where had that come from?

Her mouth went dry. "Not if anyone gets hurt."

"But what if no one does? What if the danger is perceived but not actually real, no physical trauma involved? Like the risk of being exposed. Would that kind of danger turn you on?''

Trying to ignore the weird feeling his probing prompted, she said, ''Be more specific.'' Maybe she should stop this right here, right now, but truth be told, she was getting more provoked by the minute.

''Talk to me,'' he urged her.

Annie licked her lips. Nate was always trying to get her to talk. Get her to reveal her fantasies. Get inside her head.

''C'mon, Annie,'' he urged as they turned into the alleyway. ''What would be dangerous but not? What would turn you on?''

Spotting the Harley near the building's back entrance, under the metal fire escape, she admitted, ''Last night did.''

''Creating a little steam on a rooftop wasn't really dangerous, now, was it?''

''Dangerous enough,'' she said, steaming up now, just remembering. ''Someone could have seen us. That risk of being exposed you mentioned.''

''But you didn't stop me.''

''No.''

''Why not?''

''Because I was too turned on.''

He latched on to her arm and gave her a searching look. ''Like now?''

Every nerve in her body rose up in agreeable chorus as she said, ''Yes.''

''So what are you going to do about it?'' he asked as they finally reached his motorcycle.

Heat sizzled in all her private places and some not so private, too. She wanted him to touch her again, to "do her" the way he had last night, to give her a mind-blowing orgasm. But she wanted to do him, as well.

Still she hesitated.

"C'mon, Annie, I *dare* you."

She'd never been able to resist a dare.

Swallowing hard, she pushed Nate back against the Harley parked below the fire escape. They were hidden in shadows, yet not truly protected. The alley opening was mere yards away, and despite the late hour, she knew occasional pedestrians passed by.

Any one of them could turn off the street into the alley and discover them—

Interrupting her train of thought, Nate murmured, "What do you want to do to me?"

"This," she said, pulling his face down so that she could kiss him.

Her head swam with the wonder of it, and she deepened the kiss, then interrupted it long enough to do something she'd been wanting to do since Nate had first appeared. She dipped the tip of her tongue into his cleft.

"Salty," she murmured approvingly, before kissing him again.

He leaned back against the Harley and allowed her to take the lead. Inserting a hand between them, she unzipped his leathers—first his jacket, then his pants. Her heart trilled and she had a frozen second when she thought she couldn't breathe. Gasping, she pulled away from him long enough to draw in a long, shaky breath. Then she kissed him again, and her trembling hand easily worked its way down to discover that he wasn't wearing boxers *or* briefs.

As she connected with his flesh and grasped him lightly, he groaned into her mouth. "Oh, Annie."

Moisture gathered between her thighs and her pulse beat a rapid tattoo in her throat. His erection was even larger than she'd expected. She slid her hand down its length. A pulse pressed back. He was hot and, at the very tip, wet. She rolled the bead of moisture around the tiny opening and he pressed hard into her hand.

Tearing his mouth from hers, he found her ear and whispered, "That's it, Annie. Take me all the way."

How far *was* she willing to take this? Annie asked herself, but she couldn't find a reason to stop.

The noise from the street seemed very far away. And if there had been some passerby wondering what was going on in the alley, she didn't know about it. She didn't want to.

And she didn't want to stop. She didn't want to have to rationalize about what she was doing here. Whether or not Nate was okay. Whether or not she was safe. She only knew she wanted to make him crazy for her.

Working him with her hand, she lowered herself until she was kneeling, her face level with his zipper. She nudged his thighs wider so she could get closer.

Even in the harsh blue-green light of the alley, the Harley seemed to gleam at her—a machine that was as powerful as the desire she was feeling for its night rider.

The tip of her tongue met the tip of his penis and she licked off the bead of moisture. He groaned but didn't say a word.

She licked his head, then took it in her mouth and

sucked on the soft tissue. Her pulse raced; she could hear it in her ears in direct competition with his breath, which was coming faster and louder.

The noise seemed to echo through the alley. Surely someone would hear. But the fear didn't match the excitement of surrounding him with her mouth.

She took him deeper. Faster. Harder.

He threaded his fingers through her hair and tightened his grip so that it was somewhere between pleasure and pain. She cupped him, stroked him with her mouth until he was as deep as he could go, then set up a rhythm that he couldn't resist. His fingers tangled in her hair and held her fast as he picked up the movement.

And then, with a whispered oath, he stiffened, and his pulsing into her mouth was as exciting to her as her own orgasm had been the night before.

He'd barely finished before he pulled her to her feet, kissing her deeply, certainly tasting himself. He arranged her on top of him, so that she was in his lap facing him, her legs wrapped around his back. He folded his arms around her and held her close, nuzzling her neck and stroking her hair.

Annie grew restless, breathless. Not because she was turned on—he wasn't trying to seduce her. He was holding her tenderly, as if he cared for her. The backs of her eyes grew hot, but she squeezed them tight so the unexpected moisture couldn't escape. Nate, her protector… It was a good feeling. She stayed that way, filled with a sense of wonderment that she hadn't anticipated, until his heartbeat slowed.

That's when Nate slid his hand to her breast, and Annie unwound her legs and set her feet down on the blacktop. The look in his face nearly seduced her, but, determined, she shook her head.

"Fair is fair," she said, touching him again long enough to tuck him away and zip up his pants. She wasn't unaware that he had a growing hard-on. "Besides, any more would be tempting fate."

Too conscious now of being in the open, she just wanted to get out of there, to get home, before someone caught them.

It was only when they were on the Harley, moving off, that Annie glanced back in time to see a dark figure—Harry Burdock?—meld into the shadows.

9

"I DON'T KNOW WHAT'S COME over me," Annie admitted to Nick early the next morning. "I'm acting so out of character that I'm starting to scare myself."

She'd cornered him at his place, Nick's Knack, which occupied a good-size chunk of the second floor of the six-corner commercial building and sat directly over Annie's Attic. Nick lived as well as worked here—not that it was zoned for anything but work space, as evidenced by his video equipment. Not only did Nick have his own professional videocam, but he had bought some old editing and sound equipment, as well. A ministudio occupied half of his space, while the other half was filled with metal racks and electronics.

Annie figured Nick's budget was tighter than hers or Helen's, so he was saving money by bunking in a corner on an old trundle bed. He didn't seem to mind, no doubt because he didn't spend much time here. He worked. He hung out at the cybercafé. And *cooking* was a foreign word to Nick.

Then there were his regular disappearances, Annie recalled. They kept him away from the place so often that she figured he must be secretly involved with someone he didn't want to talk about.

Kind of the way she felt about Nate.

Only she *had* to talk, *had* to make some sense of why she was doing what she was doing. She'd given Nick an edited version of her late-night tryst with Nate. Thankfully, he'd spared her the embarrassment of having to spell out the details.

"It sounds pretty simple to me," Nick said. "You're in lust with the man."

"With Nate."

"Right, that's what I said."

"No, you said 'the man.'" She wiggled around on the metal folding chair, trying to get comfortable. "I'm not in lust with Nathaniel, just with Nate." And maybe a little more than in lust with, she thought, trying not to panic. "So what am I going to do about it?"

He gave her a worried look, but didn't question her about the Clark Kent–Superman thing. All he said was "Enjoy."

"I should have known you wouldn't understand, you...you *man.*" Though she tried to sound aggrieved, she had a hard time being irritated with Nick.

"So take it to Helen," he said.

"So she can preach to me? No thanks. I was hoping for a more impartial perspective."

"You really want it, you got it." But he didn't look too comfortable as he added, "Maybe you're more than in lust. Maybe you're in love."

Annie started and felt like a rock had just settled in the pit of her stomach. "Don't be ridiculous."

"And maybe you don't want to be."

"And the reason would be...?"

Nick actually squirmed as he asked, "You're sure you want to hear this?"

Annie gave him a scathing look. "Would I have come to you if I didn't want some honesty?"

"All right, I think you're afraid."

"Of Nate?" *Maybe....*

"Of committing yourself."

She'd been in love once, and look how that had turned out. Still, she said, "I thought you were the one who said I was a one-man woman."

"No doubt in my mind," he said with a shrug. "It's *your* mind that I'm worried about."

"Why would I be afraid?"

"Once burned..."

"That was eons ago. I'm over Alan Cooper. I've been over him for years," she said, telling herself that that was not an out-and-out lie.

Alan Cooper had been the reason she hadn't given any other man a real shot at her—not that she thought it would have mattered if she had. None of them had been Nate.

"Annie, love, if you were over what Alan did to you, you would have gotten on with your life."

"I have. What do you call Annie's Attic?"

"An excuse. You've settled for your books and movies and the fantasies you create with your work rather than dealing with a real man."

"I've dated other men."

"Hah! How many did you more than kiss?"

"None of your business, Nicholas Novak!" She wasn't about to admit that she hadn't slept with anyone else, though she suspected Nick knew, anyway.

"You haven't been willing to put yourself out there because Alan was scum and you've been afraid the next guy would be scum."

That was Nick. Honest to a fault. But then she'd asked for it, Annie knew.

"Maybe it's true that I've been cautious," she admitted, "but it's also true that I just haven't met anyone that hit any buttons."

"Until Nate."

"Until Nate," she echoed.

"Now you just have to figure out what buttons those are."

Heat flushed through her at the memories. "Oh, I think I've figured it out."

"And I think that you're thinking too simplistically. I wasn't talking about the physical thing. What is it that attracts you to Nate?"

No man had ever spoken to her the way Nate had, she admitted. He touched her inner core, her true self. Maybe he was the first man who had ever looked deep enough inside her to do so.

But what she said was "His Harley." If there was anything she could blame for her uncharacteristic behavior, an inanimate object was as good a fall guy as any.

Nick shook his head. "Superficial."

"Okay. What his Harley represents."

"Which is?"

"A free spirit. Someone who lives in the moment. Takes risks." Then she remembered how it had all started, how safe and excited she'd felt from day one. "Someone who is willing to get up in the middle of the night to come to my rescue, even when I didn't exactly need rescuing."

"Your knight in shining armor."

Remembering having that exact fantasy, she said,

"As close to one as I'll ever meet. Only...he's more of a black knight."

"Because he makes you take risks."

Risks she didn't even want to think about in the light of day. "And he scares me sometimes."

"Is he the one who scares you, or is it Nathaniel?"

"Nathaniel? Not hardly. He's too conventional."

"Exactly. And he reminds you of Alan."

Annie's breath caught in her throat. She hadn't made that connection, but now that Nick had...

"Not every man's an Alan Cooper, Annie. Not every man's a piece of scum who is so bored with life that he'll turn your world upside down and think of it as a game."

It's only a game....

Nate's easily issued words still haunted her, still tainted what should be a joyful memory.

"How do I know the difference?" she asked, wanting in the worst way to get on with her life, just like Nick had prodded her to do. Why couldn't she have it all—the things romance novels promised? And why not with Nate?

"I wish I could tell you."

"I wish you could, too." Then it came to her. "Maybe you *can,* Nick, buddy."

He narrowed his gaze at her as he said, "I think you should trust your own instincts."

"I'd rather trust *yours.* I relied on my own instincts once and look what happened. I had different fantasies then. Marriage, kids, the nice house and a couple of pets. All exploded in my face." Annie swallowed hard. She didn't want to beg, but she would if she had to. Helen had raised some credible doubts, and

Nick was the protective big brother she'd never had. "I'm getting in deep, Nick, and I don't know what to trust anymore. But *your* instincts have always been good."

She gave him her best soulful look, expecting him to cave as he normally would. Though he might have his problems with the rest of the world, he could never resist helping out her or Helen in a crisis.

"Annie..."

"Nick, please. I don't want to believe anything bad about Nate, but his family does have a mobster client—charming in his own crude way, but still a mobster, and apparently only Nate can handle him. And Helen has me a little spooked about all these things that have been happening to me. My business being attacked. The mysterious notes. The photographs. The call in the night."

"Whoa, back up there. What call in the night?"

"It happened after I covered the windows. I picked up the phone and at first no one said anything. Then a voice—some guy—said I couldn't hide from him."

A pulse ticked in Nick's cheek and his expression made her catch her breath.

"Please, do this for me," she begged. *"Please."*

He didn't answer right away.

Annie shifted uncomfortably.

"All right," he finally agreed in a tight voice. "I'll ask around, see what I can find out about the man."

Clearly he was uncomfortable, but he had agreed, and that's all Annie cared about. After her wanton behavior, she needed some reassurances that she wasn't playing the fool. That her heart wasn't opening up for the first time since Alan, only to be broken once more. She wanted at least a reasonable reassurance that Nate—or Nathaniel, more precisely—wouldn't make a fool out of her in the end.

Not that she was thinking about rose-covered cottages or kids or whatever. She just wanted a relationship in which she could have not only excitement, but trust as well.

Rising from her chair, she hugged Nick. "Thanks. See you tonight at my place."

"I'll be there," he said as she made for the door. "Will Nate?"

She stopped with her hand on the knob and squeezed it harder than necessary to make it turn. "I hope so." Then, throwing open the door, she headed down the stairs.

Annie had invited Nate to the party the night before, when he'd come into her place for a few minutes. She was a little upset that he'd been noncommittal, telling her that he would have to check his calendar—a fact that bothered her as much as his quick departure had. She'd tried to excuse him, thinking he might, indeed, have other plans.

Or he could be feeling a little weird about the experience she had initiated in the alley.

Remembering the movement in the shadows, Annie took a shaky breath and stepped out onto the street. Had someone been watching them? Harry Burdock, perhaps? Or what about Clive Hardy? She wouldn't even cross Vincent Zavadinski off that list. Or maybe it had been no one. Maybe her imagination had been in high gear, like it was now.

She fancied hidden eyes followed her as she left the doorway and sprinted the several yards to her shop, which wouldn't be open for business for hours yet.

Once inside, she paused and stared out the window, as if by sheer will she could reveal the dark secrets of the now sunlit street.

Not to mention the identity of a stalker.

NATE FOUGHT WITH HIMSELF about going to Helen's birthday party. She didn't like him because she obviously thought she had his number. If only Helen knew how wrong she was…

He would have to get her a last-minute present, he decided. Unfortunately, he didn't think she was bribable. Despite his irritation with the blonde, he decided that Annie was more important than Helen's bad opinion of him.

Seeing Annie, touching her, doing unspeakable things to her to make her writhe with passion and scream out his name—things that would be so good they would drive away the last of her inhibitions—had become his obsession. And until that obsession was satisfied, he couldn't afford to miss an opportunity to be with her.

And he had to admit she was beginning to mean more to him than he'd ever imagined she could. What had started as a challenge had metamorphosed into something deeper, something more intense. Something scarier, he acknowledged. But he was ready and willing to see how far those feelings could go. And to do that, he had to stay in Annie's good graces.

To that purpose, he dressed with care—not the black leathers, but worn jeans and a silk T that she wouldn't be able to resist touching. Thinking about her hands on him, and especially about her wicked little mouth, gave him a hard-on. Though he tried to control himself, it was no use, Nate conceded.

Hopefully, the vixen would be properly flattered. He'd hardly dented his plans for her, and now was not the time for things to go awry.

"WOW, THIS IS SOME improvement," Helen said from her spot on the couch. "Who would have guessed some swaths of material over the windows could make such a difference? It's starting to look like an actual home."

Next to Helen, John Riley was pouring her a glass of wine. "Very private," he said. "Too bad it blocks the light."

"During the day, the upper windows give me plenty of light," Annie told him.

She craned her neck, looking around the large room. The space was filled with mutual friends and acquaintances from the neighborhood, most standing in the kitchen area and chatting despite the music blasting from her stereo.

"You need to do more decorating like this," Helen added. "It suits you."

"I do like it," Annie admitted as she admired the window hangings from an aesthetic point of view—not just as a source of privacy. She was trying to forget about the photographs of herself, but they haunted her, especially since the windows seemed to be the focal point of the conversation. "Actually, I have two rooms of estate-sale treasures upstairs. I keep meaning to work them down this way, but I can't seem to find the time."

"So make the time. You work too hard."

Nick snorted. "That's the pot calling the kettle black."

Annie tuned out for a moment as her two friends traded barbs.

Was Nate coming or not? He hadn't gotten back to her, but she still had hopes. She'd chosen her soft broomstick skirt and matching embroidered vest to please him.

"Let's dance," Nick said, dragging Annie to a clear area under the windows.

Once they started, others joined in, including Helen and Riley. Annie looked at them a little enviously. She would give anything to be in Nate's arms instead of Nick's.

But she wasn't going to let his absence spoil Helen's birthday, she decided, as the music ended.

"Food!" she yelled in Nick's ear, dragging him to the refrigerator.

With his help, she covered the counter and coffee table with tasty snacks from a local gourmet shop. The spinach-artichoke dip, red pepper and eggplant hummus and smoked Gouda with an assortment of crackers made a tasty-looking spread. Riley opened another bottle of wine and played bartender.

"Dig in," Annie said, taking a glass and following him back to the couch, where he took his seat next to Helen.

Riley asked, "So what other kinds of things did you get in that estate sale?"

Unable to remember a single piece of art that would fit in Gallery R, Annie said, "I doubt there's anything that would interest you."

"Try me."

"Decorative stuff, including a few paintings and watercolors, but nothing of note. Some personal things..."

"As in?" He leaned back and stretched an arm out along the couch back behind Helen.

Annie was going to have to get her friend to *spill,* as Nick so aptly put it, she decided, wishing that she was on the couch and Nate was wrapping his arm behind *her.*

"Some old costume jewelry. A salt and pepper shaker collection. A box of fancy fans." Which she was now thinking would be fun to mount on the wall closest to her bed. "A bunch of old framed photographs."

"How interesting are the frames?" Riley asked over a muffled buzzing sound that cut off abruptly.

Annie's pulse picked up. "Uh, excuse me," she said, practically running to the door. Then she slowed down purposefully and, taking a deep breath, waited for the doorbell to sound.

But the moment it did, she dragged open the door, to find Nate standing on the other side. No matter that she was irritated over the fact that he hadn't called. He was here now. Looking good enough to eat... again. And he cradled a gaily wrapped package in the crook of one arm.

"Sorry I'm late," he said. "Had to stop to get something for the birthday girl."

"Hey, no problem. We've just opened the wine."

While securing the door, she was aware of Nate flicking his gaze over her approvingly, making her glad that she'd worn something feminine and had let her hair cascade over one shoulder, loosely held by a fancy clip.

"Walk in front of me," he said softly. "I want to watch the way that material caresses you as you move."

A command that instantly made her hum all over. A glance below his waist assured her that he was having as strong a reaction to her as she was to him. Those worn jeans hid nothing! Raising her eyebrows, she blinked at him, adjusted her glasses and did as he demanded. She couldn't help herself.

Grinning happily, she rejoined her friends. "Look who I found wandering around outside."

Helen's smile was tight, but she refrained from comment.

Riley handed Nate a glass of wine. "Seeing you here tonight is something of a surprise. Our hostess wasn't exactly forthcoming about the guest list."

"Any more surprises?" Helen asked mildly.

Nate answered, "I'll see what I can do."

Annie told herself to ignore the sudden tension between the man she lusted after and her best friend. She didn't need anything spoiling the evening for her. Or for Helen, for that matter, since it was her special day.

Annie lifted her glass. "A toast," she proposed, waving the others over. "To good friends, wonderful birthdays and success and enjoyment in all our endeavors."

"Sure you didn't miss something?" Nick teased, raising his glass.

They all toasted, clinked and slipped.

Drinking and nibbling, they chatted about birthdays, trying to outdo each other with amusing stories and memories.

Busy devouring Nate with her eyes and lusting after him in her heart, Annie only half listened, wrapped up in her happiness that he was here.

"Hey, is that Rock?" Nick asked, and Annie glanced in the direction he indicated to catch her cat skulking in the shadows.

"That's the boy."

"He's put on some weight."

"He likes to eat."

Annie went after the cat and picked him up so she could show him off. But when she rejoined the others, Rock stiffened and began growling.

"Nice looking cat," Riley said, "but not too friendly, is he?"

"I don't know what's wrong with him lately." Annie tried holding him closer to calm him. "Rock, baby, it's okay. No one here is going to hurt you."

But the cat twisted in her hands while continuing to growl. Annie did the only thing she could under the circumstances—she set him down. He immediately sprinted for the safe area under her bed.

"I guess he didn't like the company," Helen stated.

Frowning, Annie said, "I guess not."

The cat's reaction put a pall on the birthday jokes, so Annie figured it was time for the cake. Going to fetch it, she lit the candles in the kitchen area, then set the chocolate butter cream confection directly in front of Helen. Everyone gathered round to sing an off-key rendition of "Happy Birthday."

"You actually put twenty-eight candles on it!"

Helen complained as she stared down at the conflagration.

"The last time I checked, that's how old you were supposed to be today."

"But if I don't blow them all out, I won't get my wish."

"Which is?" Nick asked.

"Like I would tell you."

In the end, Helen did blow out all her candles, and ate the first piece with a satisfied grin. After that, Annie lined up the presents, which Helen wasted no time in opening. Several CDs meant to be played in the café. Computer games. And there were items more personal. A leopard-print nightgown from Annie. A video Nick had edited from footage he'd shot at the grand opening of Helen's Cybercafé. A set of coffee mugs with an unusual design from Nate—really thoughtful, Annie decided. And a small piece of unframed artwork from Gallery R.

"The frames," Annie said to Riley. "Is that why you asked about them?"

"Exactly," the gallery owner admitted. "I couldn't find anything I liked to go with this."

"Then maybe I should go look for them," she offered. "I think I remember where I saw the box last."

Annie rose, and Helen asked, "You're going to do it now?"

"It'll only take a few minutes. Have another piece of cake." Chocolate cake with chocolate butter cream frosting was Helen's weakness. Noting that one couple was moving to the music once more, Annie looked from Helen to Riley and said, "Or you could always dance."

Annie started off, Nate right behind her.

"I'll go with you," he whispered in her ear, and Annie didn't argue.

The thought of a few minutes alone with him made her pulse race. They'd have time for a stolen kiss or two…or maybe more…

She led the way toward the front door and then up the wooden staircase to the landing, which had a door at each end. Certain she knew where she'd last seen the box, she headed for the door to the right, the room that adjoined the living area atrium.

No sooner had she opened the door and turned on the overhead light—a single dim bulb barely better than a nightlight—than Nate pushed her inside, twirled her around and closed the door.

"What are you doing?" Her question was punctuated by a breathless giggle.

"Helping you."

He was behind her, his arm wrapped around her body, his hard pelvis pressed against her soft behind.

Hard…the way he'd seemed to be since he'd arrived, at least whenever she'd glanced his way. She wondered if anyone else had noticed.

"Um, the boxes are behind us," she said. "So…if you can back off…"

"Uh-uh. I like where I am right now."

Though she liked it, too, Annie thought of her guests. "Later," she whispered.

"Now," he countered.

Her heart beat against her ribs. His hands slipping under her vest seemed to be trying to feel its increased beat. No, they were actually lifting her breasts from beneath. He cupped the soft flesh, flicked their tips through the silk with his thumbs.

Though heat coursed through her in waves, she said, "Nate, stop." She couldn't do this with her friends just below.

"You don't like it?"

"Of course I like it."

"Good."

He moved even closer, so that she could feel his whole body against hers. She twisted around, but merely managed to bring them both off balance. Nate gave her a tug and they fell together on a pile of material overflowing the packing boxes. Even so there was an explosion of sound that was sure to be noted by those below, even though the music was loud enough to make the floor vibrate.

Annie's laugh grew tense. "Help me up."

"I'll help you," he promised, smothering any protest with a kiss.

Annie *wanted* to protest—well, part of her did—but she wanted other things more.

Like his fingers pulling at her nipples through the thin bra. And his rigid erection pressed into the V at her thighs, which she helplessly spread for him. Seared by the sensations that shot up her spine, she arched against him and moaned into his mouth.

He was already lifting her skirts, his clever hands mesmerizing her into submission, when he murmured against her mouth, "What would make you really, really hot, Annie? Ready to explode?"

Clearly seeing Helen's disapproving expression in her mind's eye, Annie tried to find a way out of this. But then his fingers slid up her thighs and met the edge of her panties. She'd worn a thong for easier access, and now she was getting full benefit of her choice.

"That!" she gasped out, even as she thought she might be a lunatic.

Her friends were below, undoubtedly wondering about that noise. And Nate and she were lying together on broken boxes...not that she was uncomfortable in the conventional sense, since they were swathed by yards of fabric.

Nate caught her full attention by smoothing a fingertip along her cleft, but it was through the material. "This?" he whispered.

"Underneath," she heard herself say, her mind hazing over as if she'd been drugged.

"Take them off."

Alarmed by a noise from below, Annie froze. If they didn't get back downstairs in a timely fashion, everyone would *know* what she and Nate had been doing up here.

"Now," he urged her. "If you want me to turn you inside out, take them off."

"What if someone ventures up here to see what's taking us so long?"

"What if they do? C'mon, Annie, learn to live dangerously. You might like it."

His words gave her a start, but did nothing to stop the rush she felt.

She gazed at him through slitted eyes. "How dangerous are you, Nate?"

She was primed, ready. Wanting what she'd been fantasizing about for what seemed like eons.

"How dangerous do you want me to be?"

He clutched her wrists and pulled them over her head, effectively pinning her to the old draperies.

Feeling faint with desire, she asked, "Is this a game to you?"

"I know lots of games. So play with me."

Dangerous games, she thought. A man who was comfortable with a mobster certainly knew how to play them. And she seemed to be a willing participant.

"Take off your panties," he urged again, releasing her wrists so she could do so.

If she gave in, what was the worst that could happen?

"*Now,* Annie!"

Unable to fight any longer the need coursing through her, Annie lifted her hips and tugged at the material until it tore.

"Oh, no."

"Oh, yes," he murmured, his tone satisfied, his hands now busily releasing her breasts from the bra without taking off the undergarment. "Undo me."

He lifted himself slightly, but didn't stop the assault on the tender flesh of her breasts now spilling from the constricting material. Annie couldn't think clearly.

Dangerous.... Was he really? Was this an innocent game or was there more?

Even as she heard muffled laughter from downstairs, he tweaked a nipple harder and she forced her hands between them. The moment she undid the zipper—no underwear, again—he sprang free of the soft jeans. His turn to moan.

But he removed a hand from her breast long enough to reach into a pocket and place a condom in her hand. ''Put it on me,'' he urged, shoving his jeans down his hips without changing position.

''Here? Now?''

''What do you think?''

She didn't know what she had been thinking. Maybe that they would play around a little, have a few stolen thrills. A little harmless danger where no one got hurt. But this? Doing it with people below, who were by now discussing what was going on up here? That hadn't occurred to her.

Annie now thought she *must* be crazy—wild and crazy—because she ripped open the package and, with hands that trembled slightly, rolled the condom down his length.

Exploring fingers opened her, coaxed the moistness over her inner flesh. Finally, *finally,* his tip probed her wetness.

Then Nate was in her. At last. He was filling her, stroking her, loving her...

And Annie was lost.

Her awareness of the people below faded away on the other side of passion. All she knew was Nate. And *this.* Rising tension that bowed her whole body, inside out. The promise of pleasure long denied and soon to be met. With a man who meant more to her than the satisfaction she knew he would give.

Nate rolled over the piled draperies, taking her with him so that she landed on top, in a tangle of their own clothing, half on, half off.

''Ride me, Annie!'' he murmured into her ear. ''Think of the wind at your back and ride me hard.''

They were on the Harley and she was in front of him...facing him...teasing his head with her heat...

They sped out of the park and onto the streets and people turned and pointed.

She didn't care.

She slid down his length, then back up so that just the tip of him remained inside her. And then she did it again. And again. Faster. Harder.

She opened her eyes and met his gaze. He played her breasts so that she cried out in readiness.

One of his hands dipped down into the V between them. "Now," he urged, stroking her. "Now!"

Then she did cry out as she came and came and came, the sensation never seeming to end, not until she felt the pressure inside her lessen, so that she knew he'd taken the leap right beside her.

10

"WOW!" ANNIE MURMURED, collapsing on Nate. Every nerve throughout her body was alive and singing.

"You ain't seen nothing yet," he promised.

Fearing that he might try to keep that promise now, she scrambled back and only then took stock of her own disheveled state. She pulled her bra back over her breasts, saying, "I think we'd better get downstairs."

"If you insist."

Seemingly casual about it, he tugged up his jeans while rising. Caught by the beauty of his masculinity, she went all tight inside again, even as he zipped himself away from sight.

Then he swooped down and, when he straightened, held a bit of nothing in his hand. "I think you might want to do something with these."

Heat seared her neck as she stared at what was left of her panties. Grabbing them, she stuffed them in a pocket and patted it down so there was no telltale bulge.

He was grinning at her.

"What?"

"You're beautiful when you're embarrassed."

"I'm not."

"Not beautiful or not embarrassed?"

"You pick," she said, grinning back.

No one had actually called her beautiful before. Well, no one but her parents. Annie was inordinately pleased by a compliment that shouldn't have meant so much to her, not when she valued what was inside people more than what was on the outside. But Nate thought she was beautiful....

She let him take the lead down the stairs. Helen was sitting alone on the couch at the moment, her gaze perhaps a little too neutral, a little too studied, as she watched them descend. But Annie could feel disapproval coming at her in waves.

Nick was in the kitchen area, his back turned, talking intently to two other guests—it seemed that a few people had already left—but Helen was definitely watching the stairs for them.

"I thought you went up there to find some frames."

Oh, boy. "I thought I knew where the frames were, but they eluded us." Rather her memory had eluded her, once presented with an irresistible distraction.

"For a very long time," Nick said, turning toward them, for once not sounding amused. "We were about to send out a search party."

What was wrong with him? she wondered. He'd been all for her getting closer to Nate. Had the fact that she'd asked him to check Nate out changed his attitude to the other man?

The door behind Annie opened as she turned to her friend, not wanting her to be angry. "Sorry, Helen. I'll look for those frames tomorrow."

Riley moved past Annie to sit on the couch next to a yawning Helen.

"Sure. Whatever," Helen said. "But I'm afraid I'm going to have to break up the birthday-fest and get some sleep."

"So soon?"

"Uh, you were up there longer than you think."

Annie felt her cheeks flush again. Thankfully, Nate had moved away from her so she could at least breathe properly.

Helen started to gather her presents, and Riley lent a hand.

"I think we'd better all call it a night," Nick said, his expression odd.

The few other guests agreed, said their good-nights and left.

When Helen picked up her new video, Nick said to Annie, "By the way, I finished that dance video for Club Undercover over on Milwaukee. Let me know if you want to catch it some night this week."

"Definitely," Annie said.

Arms full of presents, Riley said, "Great get-together, Annie. Thanks for thinking of me."

"I'm glad you could make it."

Helen hugged her. "Thanks, Annie." She glanced over at Nate, who hung back from the group. "Take care of yourself, okay?"

Nick bent close and kissed Annie on the cheek. "And I want to talk to you tomorrow," he said for her ears only. "Alone."

That sounded ominous. Trying to hide her worry, she glanced from him to Nate, who was trying to get a look under her bed, where Rock still hid.

Worrying about the cat—he'd been acting so strangely lately—she showed her friends to the door. And by the time they were outside, Nate had caught up to her.

Her pulse ticked in a rapid beat. But if Annie had hopes of a repeat performance of what had gone on upstairs, she was doomed to disappointment.

"I need to get going as well," Nate told her.

Because they had no potential audience? No element of danger to spice up the moment? she wondered as he pressed a soft, quick kiss to her lips.

"I'll call you," he promised.

Words that every woman dreaded. Would he really call her now that he'd gotten what he wanted from her?

But this was Nate, she reminded herself, not Alan Cooper. Still, she fought the sick feeling that shot through her.

"I look forward to it," she responded.

Like a lovesick teenager, she watched him get on his Harley and ride off into the night.

Lovesick? Could Nick be right?

Not wanting to analyze too deeply, she tried to enjoy the now. A few minutes later, soaping herself in the shower, touching the places tender from their exciting lovemaking, she couldn't help but relive the stolen moments with Nate.

Would there be more of them?

Though she tried to wash away the taste of fear, it lingered in her mouth. But this fear was different. It couldn't be assuaged by a locked door or the presence of other people.

This wasn't fear for her physical safety, but for her heart.

EARLY THE NEXT MORNING, the other kind of fear welled up in her all over again.

Fear and anger.

Having decided that she had too many things to do at the shop to stay home and relax—as if she ever did—she'd set out for Annie's Attic, though this was the one day a week it was closed to business. As she approached the six corners, she'd noticed a couple of people with flyers in hand, but it wasn't until she got closer to her shop that she realized the sidewalk was littered with them.

She bent to pick one up....

"You're sure you didn't see anyone handing these out?" she now asked Helen's employees, who were working hard to keep up with the busy early morning traffic at the café. She'd been so upset upon reading the damned thing that she'd headed right over there to show her friend.

"Nope, sorry," one of them said as he filled a customer's order.

"Who has time to pay attention to anything but work?" asked the other.

Hands trembling, Annie read the flyer again.

Annie's Attic
For Expensive Trash
Annie Wilder,
Proprietress and Slut

"Sit," Helen said. "I'll get you some herbal tea to calm you down."

"I don't need tea!" Annie argued as she sat. "I need a damn name!"

"Try Alderman Zavadinski."

Annie looked up to see John Riley, steaming commuter mug in hand, standing nearby.

"You saw him handing these out?"

"No, but he drove by a little while ago—very slowly and with his window rolled down. He looked like he was enjoying himself."

"Bastard!" Annie cried. "He really is trying to drive me out of business."

"This will backfire on him, just like the last time," Helen predicted.

Not that it would make Annie feel any better. "I don't understand. I'm just trying to run an honest business. What does Zavadinski think he can get out of it?" She was getting hysterical. "Does he really think he can beef up his political career on my hide? Maybe eventually run for mayor on an antitrash, antislut campaign, citing driving me out of business as his big accomplishment during his term as alderman?"

"Calm down," Helen said. "If you ask me, he's probably just a lust-filled, middle-aged man who can't get it up anymore, and your shop drives that fact home to him."

"Maybe he's lusting after you," Riley added.

"After *me?* I'm no sexpot."

"Maybe he sees beyond the outer coverings and is lusting after what's inside your mind."

"I'll give him a piece of my mind!" Annie said, flying to her feet.

"Whoa, hold on," Helen said. "You can't be serious."

"Oh no? Just watch me."

With that, she marched out the door, ignoring Helen's pleas that she take time to think things through before acting. Annie didn't need time. She needed to speak her mind.

And so she charged down Milwaukee Avenue the two blocks to the alderman's storefront office.

"Is he in?" she asked the dark-haired young woman at the front desk, who glanced down at her appointment calendar.

"And you would be?"

"An angry constituent." She maneuvered past the reception desk.

The young woman yelled after her, "Hey, you can't go in there!"

"Watch me!" Annie said, throwing open the door and crossing the room to face down her archenemy.

Zavadinski was smiling—*smiling!*—as if he'd been waiting for her.

"How can I help you, Miss Wilder?"

"You can stop dishing out this trash!" She slammed down the flyer on his desk.

"Oh, I don't need one of those. I've already seen it."

"I'm sure. Did you have these made up yourself or did you get one of your flunkies to do your dirty work?"

"I'm not the one doing the dirty work, Miss Wilder. I believe that's *your* specialty."

Annie wanted to hit him. Or at least throw something. She stood there trembling with fury, feeling vindicated and yet foolish. Helen had been right. She should have thought twice before confronting the bastard. What good had it done? Even the element of surprise hadn't gotten him to confess.

He was playing with her, she thought.

"Two can play at this game, Alderman. You go ahead and ruin my business and I'll have so much time on my hands that I might have to get involved in the upcoming campaign...making sure that you lose the election!"

His silver-threaded brows drew together and his round face grew ruddier than usual. "Is that a threat?"

"Call it a warning. Don't mess with me. You don't know who I know."

With that she spun around and marched out of his office without looking back.

Who she knew, indeed!

Gloria's cousin Julio, perhaps? Or maybe Nate's mobster client. Neither of whom she would consider consulting, of course.

Yes, it had been a threat—a big, fat, empty one.

"I GOT THE SCOOP on Nathaniel Bishop," Nick said later that morning, when he came downstairs to find her in her shop doing boring paperwork.

She was sitting behind her desk, and he perched on its corner. "Already? That was fast." Her mouth went dry. "So what is it?"

"His connections with the mob go deeper than he lets on."

"What? Please don't tell me he's a hit man or something."

"Nothing that drastic. But it looks as if he's into them for a big piece of change."

"Gambling?"

"Real estate. This building for one."

"He's a front man?"

"All I know is that he didn't get a conventional mortgage for his properties," Nick admitted. "He got funding from private sources."

"And you're sure those sources are mob connected?"

"No, not sure. It's just the talk."

"Whose talk?"

Nick didn't answer right away. Then he said, "Someone I trust," and she could see that he wasn't going to give more away.

"So what am I supposed to conclude from this information?" she asked. "That Nate is connected to the mob and therefore responsible for the scary things that have been happening to me?"

"I just want you to be careful. I love you and don't want anything bad happening to you. I didn't want to do this, Annie, but you pushed. And now I'm sorry I don't have the right answers for you."

"I did push. And now I have more to think about than I want." She sighed. "Why is this so difficult?"

"This?"

"Life, I guess."

A cop-out. She'd meant love, of course. But she couldn't say the word. It was too new, too untested, and she was too uncertain. She couldn't admit what she was feeling, certainly not to her friends, not when she didn't want to admit it to herself.

What if Nick had stumbled onto the truth? A truth

that went a lot deeper than shady financing for Cornerstone Realty?

"HI, BEAUTIFUL."

Annie's heart thumped at the familiar voice on the other end of the phone line. It was midafternoon and she was almost caught up with her work.

"Hi, Nate," she murmured, putting the computer on standby.

"I've been thinking about you."

Though she wanted to ask why he hadn't called earlier, she bit her tongue lest she sound too eager. "Me, too," she said lightly. "I mean, I was thinking about you."

Only not all good thoughts, after what Nick had told her. She'd been in a spin off and on ever since.

"Can I see you tonight?"

Could he? Should she? Doubts warred with what she wanted. Yet Nick hadn't had anything concrete. Only rumors. And what if they'd been on the money? That didn't necessarily mean Nate had done anything illegal. That didn't make him a bad person.

"What did you have in mind?" she asked cautiously.

"I thought you might like to check out Nick's video at Club Undercover."

Figuring Nick might even be there, that seemed like a safe enough date. If she wanted safe.

"Dance music doesn't start till late," she warned him. "Are you sure you don't need to be up bright and early in the morning again?"

"I'll take a power nap," he said. "I promise not to run out on you early tonight."

That sounded like a loaded promise to her.

"I'll pick you up at home at nine. And Annie..."

"Mmm?"

"Don't wear any underwear tonight."

With that, Nate hung up, leaving Annie a little startled and a lot more titillated.

Did she dare?

Done with her paperwork, she decided the display window was next.

She'd played out this scenario. So she gathered a gauzy swath of material to hang across the window. The see-through cloth would partially camouflage it rather than close it off altogether. Butcher paper would be more opaque, but it was too utilitarian. Annie wanted sexy. She wanted customers to wonder what in the world she intended to do with the new display. She wanted them to salivate, and then when they saw the merchandise, to buy, buy, buy.

The only problem was that she hadn't yet decided what exactly she wanted to do with the new display.

Her being harassed by Zavadinski and his goons made her want to make this new window even hotter than the last. She would have to think about it a bit more.

Hot, hot, hot....

As she worked, her mind wandered back to Nate and his plans for her. *Don't wear any underwear tonight.* Did he intend to "do her" on the dance floor in the middle of a crowd? Though she had to draw the line somewhere, she couldn't help but fantasize a little....

They danced in a frenzy until their bodies were covered in sweat. Then the lights dimmed and the music slowed and they were in each other's arms, in a world of their own.

Subtly, he worked his clothing free and lifted the front of her skirt. They were so close together, no one could tell what was going on.

But she could. She felt his erection. Felt his tip probe between her folds. She melted inside, wet him with her passion.

When she couldn't stand it any longer, he danced her into the shadows, into the darkest corner, from which they could see everything but no one could really see them. He lifted her so that she was balanced back against a table.

And then he entered her, and within a matter of seconds, made her come.

Annie snapped out of the fantasy with a start and tended to the material she was in the middle of hanging. Of course, she would never do such a thing. Nor would Nate, she was certain. Or was she?

No matter what Nick had told her, she couldn't wait to see the man who inspired her fantasies.

Just then she looked up to see someone standing outside the shop. When she realized it was Clive Hardy, her skin crawled. His last purchase had been only days ago, and here he was back again. And he was pressed to the windowpane, staring at her through the gauzy material....

He pointed first to her, then to the door, as if he expected her to open it for him.

Annie's throat tightened. She indicated the Closed sign in the corner of the window.

He shook his head and pointed to the door again. He was insisting she let him in.

He might be her best customer, but he made her too uncomfortable to want to be alone with him. She shook her head.

Expression furious, he thumped his fist against the pane, making her jump back.

Her temper flared.

She shot to the door and unlocked it, but didn't open it more than she had to. He was there in an instant, practically in her face. And he shoved his foot between the door and the jamb so she couldn't close it if she wanted to. She shoved her own foot on the other side.

"Mr. Hardy, what do you think you're doing?"

"Trying to get in to make my purchases, of course." He gave the door a push, but she held it fast.

"We're not open today, as you can see by the sign."

"Signs are for other people."

"No, signs are for you, too."

"You mean you're not going to let me in?" he asked in a whiny, demanding tone.

"I am not."

"But I *need* to come in. *Now.* Leslie has to have more of your lingerie. And we could use some of those toys you sell. I'm sure you could recommend something I...*she* would like."

Annie's skin crawled, but she forced a polite smile. "I'm not open for business. Period. Not even to you." Especially not to him. "Please come back tomorrow."

He stared at her for a moment and his lips thinned. In a low voice that reminded her of the one on the phone the other night, he said, "You'll be sorry, Annie."

You can't hide from me....

Her heart thundered as she watched him stomp away.

As she tried to work on the window, Clive Hardy's warning echoed in her head over and over. What would he do to make her sorry? she wondered. Or what would he do next?

She simply couldn't concentrate. Finally, she gave up and called it a day.

Before going home, she returned some supplies to the building's janitor closet, then washed up there, as she usually did after working on displays.

Standing next to the sink, Annie looked down to find a short stack of magazines sitting on a pile of boxes. Girlie magazines. She wondered who had left them there. As freethinking as she was, she'd never liked the idea of these rags, at least not the hard-core kind.

The top one was open to the centerfold. A young woman with long dark hair posed in see-through lingerie, with her legs spread and her fingers...

Reminded of the photo someone had taken of her in a similar position, Annie flushed with embarrassment. Not wanting to think further about the magazines or their possible owner, she turned on the water.

One of the other tenants was certainly being noisy. Even over the stream of water, she heard the person clunking around nearby. She soaped her hands, shut out the sounds and thought about Nate and what she should wear for him tonight. It had to be something delicious, and she knew exactly the dress that would do it for him.

Caught up in anticipation, she wasn't prepared for a sudden boom behind her. Nearly jumping out of her skin, she whirled around to find the door had slammed shut.

That was enough to scare the bejesus out of anyone, Annie thought, quickly drying her hands on a paper towel and stepping over to the door.

Which wouldn't open.

The doorknob turned, but nothing happened. As far as she knew, the door couldn't actually lock trapping someone inside. Thinking her hands must be too damp to get a good grip and turn the knob fully, she wiped them on her jeans and tried again.

The knob turned easily, but nothing happened.

Somehow, Annie realized, the door had locked shut behind her.

11

"JUST GREAT!"

At least other people were in the building, this being rush hour on a Monday. And at least one person was close by, from all indications. No need to panic. She banged on the door.

"Hello? Anyone out there? I'm stuck!"

If she thought someone was going to come to her rescue, she had another think coming. Whoever had been banging around in back had obviously left. Annie pounded until her hands were sore, called out until her voice was raw. The small enclosed room had grown stuffy and hot. Sweat was running down her neck and back.

Taking a break to ease her discomfort, she ran the cold water, wet her arms and neck and took a drink from a cupped hand. Then she looked around for something that might help get her out of her predicament. Too bad she didn't have a cell phone, she thought, or she could call Nick or Helen to come back here and release her. But she was creative, and this was a janitor's closet, after all.

A shelf revealed a box of tools, including several screwdrivers and a pair of pliers. Giving the door a long, hard look, she knew what she had to do.

It was only when she had the bottom hinge half off

that it occurred to her the door slamming shut might not have been an accident. *What if someone had closed it purposely, to trap her inside?*

She tried to shake away the notion, but as she got the first hinge apart, the idea took seed.

Why would someone do it? What would he have to gain?

He? Her stalker?

Licking her lips, Annie stood in indecision for a moment.

What if he was still there, waiting? But for what? If he'd planned on doing something to her, surely he wouldn't have locked her inside the room by herself. He would have attacked her.

Unless the point was to scare her, a little voice in her head contributed.

He'd certainly succeeded in doing that. And whoever this guy was, he was a coward, hiding in shadows, behind camera lenses and telephones.

Clive Hardy? She would bet that was his style, and he'd warned her that she would be sorry...

It could be Hardy. He could have gotten back here through one of the businesses—maybe Helen's Cybercafé. Or he might have found the alley door unlocked or ajar. Sometimes tenants left and didn't secure it properly. Yeah, Annie could imagine the whiny client sneaking around back and waiting for his opportunity to do mischief.

Deciding she wouldn't let a coward stop her, she attacked the second hinge with a vengeance and soon had it free. Then, wedging two large screwdrivers between the door and the jamb, she pried open the door enough to see a bit of the area on the other side. If anyone was there she couldn't see him.

Annie struggled with the door—it was metal and heavy. She might be small, but she was tough, she told herself, inching it open.

"If you're still there, you bastard, you'd better run before I get out of here," she warned, "or I'll make mincemeat out of you!"

"Then maybe I'd better not help you," a deep voice answered from the other side.

Annie froze. That wasn't Clive Hardy. That was—

"That you, Miss Wilder?" Harry Burdock poked his head in the opening, then took over and had the door freed in a minute. "What the heck happened here?"

Heart pounding, she backed up fast. "I got locked in," she said, waiting to see his reaction. Surely a security guard would know that shouldn't have been possible. But Burdock didn't comment.

"Good thing I came along when I did then."

"Right."

He set the door next to the sink. "You okay?"

"Fine. Thank you."

The stack of magazines caught his eye. He picked up the spread and looked from it to her and then back again. "You kinda look like her, you know?"

Eeow! Surely whoever had been admiring the centerfold hadn't had *her* in mind. She gave the security guard a closer look and swore he was leering at her. Was that *his* magazine? Had he left that centerfold purposely for her to find?

When she edged toward the door, he didn't try to stop her. "Got to go," she muttered.

He grinned from ear to ear and focused his attention back on the magazine. "You have a good night, now."

That's what she'd been hoping for, but now the night felt as if it might be fraught with unknown dangers.

She hailed a taxi and spent the entire ride staring out the back window, but no matter how hard she looked, she couldn't see anyone following.

Even a long soak in her tub, with Rock looking on from the sink like a furry vulture, didn't wash away the uneasy sensations stirred up by the janitor closet incident.

Clive Hardy. Was he the one? Her stalker?

What about Harry Burdock?—was so convenient that he'd been on the spot to "rescue" her. And the way he'd leered at her with that magazine in hand had tied her stomach in knots.

Not that it hadn't already been in knots from her face-to-face encounter with Vincent Zavadinski that morning, although she didn't suspect the alderman of more than trying to destroy her business. But hadn't that been enough for one day?

She discussed the possible stalkers with Rock but, as usual, the cat didn't seem to have an opinion. At least he was out and about and acting normal, which was more than she could say for the way she was feeling.

A little strung out, she concentrated on her date. The rest could wait until morning to be dissected. Seeing Nate would make her feel better, she decided.

To that end, she dressed in a new garment she had never had the inclination to wear before tonight—an ankle-length, slim, red-hot dress that molded itself to her every curve. Heeled ankle boots, and a fat belt and matching bracelet made up of mah-jongg pieces, finished the outfit. After splashing her face with a bit more color than usual, she gathered myriad wisps of hair from around her face and fastened them to one side with a small ivory comb. Waves tumbled down her back to her bra line—or would have if she'd been wearing one.

Nate wouldn't be able to resist her, she had just decided, when the bell buzzed and shocked her system. Her pulse raced and her breath came in uneven little spurts as she headed for the entryway. Odd that she hadn't heard the Harley, though.

When she swung open the door, Annie realized it was because the bike was nowhere in sight.

Nor was Nate.

It was Nathaniel who stood there, grinning down at her.

AS NATE WATCHED Annie's expression change—going from anticipation to disappointment—his own smile faded.

He didn't understand her.

But that didn't stop him from admiring her.

Eyes traveling down her diminutive length, all the way to the high-heeled ankle boots, he murmured, "Great look."

If she was wearing any underwear, he would give away his Harley.

"Thanks, Nathaniel. Nice suit."

The words were right, the tone wasn't. A thousand-dollar suit didn't impress her. And she was calling him Nathaniel again, he realized. No doubt she would rather see him in his leathers, which seemed to make her feel more comfortable and relaxed enough to call him Nate.

Nate acknowledged the dissatisfaction that made him feel. He would take her anywhere, anytime, no matter what she was wearing. It was the woman who counted, in his mind, and he couldn't get enough of this one, no matter how she presented herself. That thought was unsettling. He'd always been able to do without before, but Annie was proving herself unique to him in every way. She could be soft and vulnerable or smart and snappy, depending on her mood. Inside of her, a number of women hid, he decided, all waiting to be freed. He looked forward to every encounter.

"Ready to go?" he asked, indicating the car parked at her curb.

Annie glanced at the Acura, murmured, "Mmm-hmm," grabbed a tiny purse and pulled the long strap over her head and across her body. When she stepped outside, she didn't kiss him or even touch him. Instead she carefully and not-so-subtly avoided him altogether, turning her back on him to lock the door.

Nate didn't like what was happening. He was getting the same vibes from her that he'd gotten when they'd gone to the family dinner.

What was her problem?

Most women would love to ride in a luxury car, love to be with a man who was obviously ready to spend big bucks on her. But Annie wasn't most women. Part of why he was fascinated by her, he told himself.

Just let the negative feelings slide....

Club Undercover was a five-minute ride from her place, and Nate used the silence to plan his strategy. He *would* get through to her, overcome this setback, if it was the last thing he did tonight!

Upon arrival, he turned his keys over to a car jockey and placed a hand on Annie's waist. He felt her stiffen a bit, but she didn't move away as he guided her inside and down the stairs to the cavernous, dark, smoky space.

Canned music was being piped throughout. A few people were already on the dance floor, but many couples and more singles were reconnoitering for tables or bar stools, claiming their space for the coming hours.

Nate had already made arrangements for the best seat in the house, one of the reserved tables away from the crowd. Only three booths sat on a rise overlooking the rest of the club, each with a perfect view of the dance floor. The curved middle booth was cozy and dark but for the array of candles of various heights decorating the mirrored table.

"We certainly have space up here," Annie said.

"I thought you would like the privacy."

"Mmm," she murmured, turning her head to watch the dancers.

This wasn't the Annie with whom he'd counted on spending the evening. This Annie was distant, practically ignoring him. The fact got to Nate.

But solving problems was his specialty—at least in business. He wasn't going to make less of an effort with his personal life. Before he was done with her, Annie wouldn't care what he wore or what he drove. She would be his, anytime, anywhere.

As for right now, he wasn't about to let her off the hook by allowing her to ignore him. He placed a hand over hers and asked, "Did Nick say what time his video would be played?"

"All night." Annie casually freed her hand and fussed with her hair. "He chose hundreds of images and then randomized them in the editing process, so they're used dozens of times in different ways with different effects."

"And he can make a living at this?"

"Nick has all kinds of projects," she admitted, finally turning her full attention back to Nate. "Some he does to pay expenses, some because he gets artistic pleasure from doing them. That was the idea of our starting our own businesses in the first place."

Was she warming up to him or was he imagining it? Nate wondered.

He again slipped a hand over hers, and while Annie didn't pull it away this time, neither did she melt at his touch. And that's what he wanted her to do.

Melt. For him.

And not just physically, he realized. He wanted her to melt inside, too. He wanted her to look at him with that special softness in her eyes, no matter if he was wearing his leathers or a business suit.

A waitress with hair that glinted as deep a blue as did her shiny blouse came over to take their drink order. Nate requested a bottle of champagne and Annie didn't object.

Maybe plied with a bit of bubbly, she would relax....

Throughout the club, customers were settling in, waiting for the deejay. It was still relatively quiet in the place, compared to what it would be like once the dance music and the crowd were in full swing.

And since Annie seemed determined to resist his charm as long as he was wearing a suit, Nate figured he might as well make small talk. "So how was your day off?"

"I spent it playing catch-up at the store."

"Did you?"

"All but the window. I couldn't concentrate after Clive Hardy showed up."

"Who?"

"A customer who kind of gives me the creeps."

"An oddball, huh? He's not a real problem, though, right?"

"I don't know. Maybe…"

Nate was getting a feeling he didn't particularly like. "What kind of problem?" He didn't need the outside world to complicate matters now.

"Um, I think…"

"Yes, what?"

"I think he may be stalking me."

IF ANNIE EXPECTED Nathaniel to show shock or outrage, she was disappointed. His puzzled expression seemed a mild reaction to such an announcement.

"Stalker? Are you kidding?"

"Right. I always joke about being stalked."

Annie watched him carefully. She'd decided to bring the stalker situation into the open with him. He had a right to defend himself, even if he didn't know that he was a candidate for the position. Even if he was a very distant candidate, nominated by Helen.

The waitress was back with their bottle of champagne and made a big production of opening it. Nathaniel took a taste and nodded in approval, so she filled their glasses and then hurried off to serve another customer.

Annie took a sip from her glass as Nathaniel scooted closer. He picked up the discussion where they'd left off.

''More photographs?'' he asked. ''Is that what this stalking thing is about?''

''Photographs?'' Thinking about what had gone on between her and Nate the night before, she said, ''Lord, I hope not!'' and took a larger gulp of her champagne.

''But the photographs from the other night are obviously part of it,'' Nathaniel said, as he topped up her glass. ''What else has you so spooked?''

''Seductive letters from an admirer, and a late-night phone call. Things have been happening at the store, and I have a general feeling of someone watching me. And, no, I am not the paranoid type. If anything, just the opposite.''

''Have you told anyone else about all this?''

''Just Nick and Helen.''

''Not the authorities?'' he asked intently.

''I don't have the energy to try to get them to believe me. I mean, I haven't been hurt, and other than getting locked in the janitor's closet—''

''When did that happen?'' he asked, interrupting.

''Today. I figured it was Clive Hardy, who tried forcing his way into the store, even though I told him it was closed and I wouldn't open up just to suit him. He's a little...unusual. Okay, odd. Anyway, he said I would be sorry and then I got locked in the closet.''

"How?" Nate muttered, more to himself than to her. "I didn't think that was possible."

"I didn't, either."

"But you did get out somehow," he said, "because here you are with me."

"I dismantled the hinges. And then Harry Burdock showed up in time to help get the door out of the way." Annie sighed. "To tell the truth, I've been wondering about your security guard, too."

"Burdock?"

"I told you I thought I saw him hanging around my place the night I got those photographs. Did you ever talk to him about it?"

"Sorry." Nathaniel's expression was as apologetic as his tone. "I dropped the ball on that one."

And yet he seemed more thoughtful than concerned, Annie noticed. Did he believe she was overreacting? Was she? Had Helen spooked her into putting things in the worst possible light?

Annie went back to her champagne and he to his.

"Welcome to Club Undercover!" a voice suddenly boomed as the music went low. Dressed in black with red accents, his long dark hair also streaked with red, the deejay took center stage on the dance floor. "Hot, hot, hot—that's the key word for the night. I'm the Dark Prince and your guide on this sensual musical journey. Now follow me...and let's see what you've got!" he yelled before launching himself up the stairs to his booth.

Annie downed the last of the champagne in her glass and let Nathaniel pour her another. She was starting to feel the bubbles going to her head, but she was also relaxing in his company. No harm in that. Who wanted to feel uptight all night?

Dancers started wandering down onto the floor as the music blasted through the club once more. And for a moment, Annie was caught, brought back to her reverie about Nate and the hot time she'd imagined....

Which Nathaniel interrupted when he said, "I heard something about a flyer this morning."

Annie blinked, fighting a sudden surge of resentment that she wasn't with the man she'd fantasized about. She took another sip of champagne.

"More of Zavadinski's nonsense in his campaign against me," she said, detailing the flyer's contents and her subsequent visit to the alderman.

"You're sure Zavadinski was behind it?"

"He didn't admit as much, but, well, who else could it have been?"

"If you do have a stalker..."

Annie started. "You think one person could be responsible for everything?"

"Not necessarily."

"Then why bring it up?"

"Just thinking out loud." Before she could respond, he grabbed her hand and pulled her up out of her seat. "Let's dance before there's no more room on the floor."

The last thing Annie wanted was to dance with Nathaniel, but she didn't seem to have a choice unless she made a scene. She dragged her heels, then swallowed hard and gave over. One dance to some hip-hop wouldn't kill her, after all.

A moment later, they were wending their way

through the crowd of dancers when the music switched to the exotic, electronic sounds of Enigma.

Uh-oh.

Once she was in Nathaniel's arms, Annie became mesmerized by the music, so heavy with sexual overtones; caught by the breathy moans of the female singer, who clearly sounded as if she were in the throes of passion. Trying to concentrate on the video, on Nick's work, wasn't any better. It seemed that her buddy had a growing fascination with erotic images.

Suddenly, the club fantasy came back to her in startling clarity....

Nate spinning her...their bodies tightly locked together...his erection secretly seeking entrance...

Annie fought the images, the mood, because she didn't want to be tricked into letting down her guard. It wasn't Nathaniel she wanted, she reminded herself. Nate should be here, holding her, inspiring her and making love to her.

But it didn't seem to matter what she wanted; her body betrayed her. *The champagne,* she decided. The drink was loosening her inhibitions and fuzzing her mind, making her vulnerable. Even as she fought it, heat spiraled through her. Her mouth went dry and she licked her lips.

Focus, she told herself. *Focus on something nonsexual.*

The other dancers. That was it. She would study them. She compared hair colors—what she could see of them in the dim light—and unusual styles. She dissected so-called fashion statements, counted the number of platform shoes under teetering dancers.

She counted eyebrow piercings and nose rings. She made an inventory of tattoos.

Anything so that she didn't have to admit to an attraction she didn't want or need. Nate was enough for her. She couldn't take on Nathaniel, as well.

Realizing she was quickly losing the battle on a purely physical level, she decided if she had been smart, she would have ordered iced tea. Determined to stop this cold before it got her into trouble, Annie pulled herself from his arms and indicated she wanted to return to their seats.

While Nathaniel didn't look too happy, he let her take the lead. She practically ran up the stairs as if she could leave her physical reaction to him behind. When she slid into the booth, he slid right next to her. Too close.

"Tired already?" he murmured, placing his hand on her knee through the slit in her skirt.

Squirming in her seat, Annie desperately sought a way out of this. "I'm not as young as I used to be," she said, a prelude to suggesting they leave.

Only being alone with Nathaniel might be worse. What if, as long as the champagne was having this liberating effect, she couldn't control herself? The thought horrified her.

"Not young," he echoed, his hand straying higher, to vulnerable thigh territory. "Says who?"

Waves of sensation washed through her as she fought herself and indicated the dancers. "Look at me and look at them. They're babies."

"They have to be at least twenty-one to get in here—unless they have fake identification, of course."

"All right. So they're legal." Thankful that her skirt was too tight for him to go higher, that he gave up at least for the moment and let her be, she said, "But they're still free to express themselves without worrying what people think. They're brave to wear their insides for everyone to see."

"Or they're hiding their real selves behind disguises," Nathaniel countered.

Was he? Annie wondered. Which was the disguise and which was the real him?

OVERWHELMED WITH RELIEF that she'd gotten away from Nathaniel without compromising herself, Annie undid the mah-jongg belt and hung it from a hook in her closet. Actually, as if he'd felt her tightening up when he'd gotten her home, he hadn't tried anything; he'd merely brushed her lips with his and wished her good-night.

How peculiar. "Why didn't he push a little?" she asked Rock.

The cat yawned in disinterest.

Not that she would have liked Nathaniel pushing, she decided. She just wondered. And the champagne was still doing her thinking. Not to mention keeping her a bit unsteady, she realized as Rock curled himself around her legs.

She lifted him, kissed his fuzzy forehead and put him on the counter as she let the dress drop to the floor, and stepped out of it.

That's when the phone rang, and standing nude but for her bracelet and heeled boots, she froze.

It rang again.

Thinking maybe it was Nate calling, Annie

couldn't still the flutter of excitement that shot through her. Maybe her evening wasn't over, after all.

Breasts tight, the warmth of anticipation curling between her thighs, she hurried to the counter and picked up the receiver.

"Hello," she said breathlessly.

And was instantly on edge when no one responded at the other end.

"Whoever this is—"

Her indignation was cut off by the sound of a familiar voice saying, *"C'mon, Annie, learn to live dangerously. You might like it."*

"Nate?"

"How dangerous are you, Nate?"

That was her voice! Gripping the receiver hard, she gaped.

"How dangerous do you want me to be?"

"Is this a game to you?"

"I know lots of games. So play with me."

Annie couldn't believe it. She was standing here in the nude, listening to a recorded conversation of herself having sex with Nate!

"Take off your panties," he was saying. *"Now, Annie!"*

Horrified, she listened to her *"Oh, no!"* and recalled the panties tearing in her hand. Frantically, Annie looked around now for something with which to cover herself.

"Oh, yes. Now undo me."

"Nate, you're scaring me," she said into the phone. "Stop this!"

Or was it Nate? she wondered as his voice murmured, *"Put it on me."*

"Here? Now?"

"What do you think?"

What *had* she been thinking?

And how had this recording been made? Annie wondered, anger warring with fear.

"Ride me, Annie! Think of the wind at your back and ride me hard!"

Had whoever it was listened while she and Nate had come together in a single burst of brilliance?

Disgusted, she slammed down the receiver, then took it off the hook while she picked up her dress and wrapped it around her body, an impromptu towel. Then she dialed Nate.

At the other end, the phone rang and rang and rang until the answering machine kicked in. Wondering why he wasn't there to answer in person—surely he'd had enough time to get home by now—Annie hung up without leaving a message.

Had her stalker gotten into her home and wired it? Had he listened while they'd been having sex or had he savored it later, maybe masturbating while listening?

What was to say he wasn't here now?

She looked around wildly and realized she couldn't stay here alone. Not tonight.

WHEN WOULD SHE COME to her senses and see him for what he was?

Disconnecting the cell phone and stopping the tape, he sat in the car and watched her lit windows as she moved around her place. He didn't have to see her to imagine her undressing. He didn't even have to look at the photographs.

Her image was burned into his brain. Her looks, her gestures, the tone of her voice. All of her. She was like a recurring fever that he couldn't shake.

Waiting for it all was getting more difficult than he had imagined. In the meantime, he'd found a way to entertain himself. And her.

She liked the kinky stuff, he thought, fingers tracing the Spycorder in his hand.

And he was just the man to give it to her.

12

"YOU CALLED THE POLICE? Finally!" Helen said, leaning over to hug Annie after she'd revealed all to her friends over early morning coffee.

"For all the good it will do me," Annie muttered, hating that she'd had to tell the authorities about the taped sex talk and turn over the letters and photographs. Well, all but the one.

"Great attitude," Nick said from the other side of the table. "They did take the report, though, right?"

"Right. And they even seemed somewhat supportive until they asked me if I suspected anyone in particular. I told them about Clive Hardy and Harry Burdock. And then I made the mistake of mentioning Vincent Zavadinski."

Nick's eyebrows shot up. "Uh-oh. Supporters of the alderman?"

"I'm afraid so."

"What about our landlord?" Helen demanded. "Did you mention him?"

"Not as a suspect, no!" Annie said.

"You don't think that *he* could have recorded your little tryst?"

Annie had been mortified having to reveal all, but hiding things from her friends wouldn't get her anywhere, she figured. Still, she couldn't believe that Nate would do this to her.

"If he had a recording device on him, then he hid it very cleverly," Annie stubbornly insisted. "Those jeans didn't hide much, believe me."

Helen shuddered. "Let's not go there."

"And he couldn't have planted a bug in that room, because he wouldn't have known we were going to be up there."

Heck, she hadn't known she would volunteer to look for picture frames.

"So then how?" Helen asked.

"One of the police officers told me there are all kinds of spy-type devices available to the public now. The pervert could have been sitting in some car right outside the building using one." That she could have looked out her window at the bastard without knowing what he was doing creeped her out. "Besides, I trust Nate. I would trust him with my life!"

"Well, you just may be doing that, honey," Helen said, her expression worried. "Have you spoken to him about this?"

Annie shook her head. "I called him first, but there was no answer. I didn't want to leave a message. Then when the police took the report, I had to identify him as being the other person on the tape, of course. So I figure he must know about it by now."

"You didn't give the guy a heads-up?" Nick asked, sounding horrified. "Coward!"

"I know. I should have tried calling him again when they left. He probably won't even want to see me after the police question him."

"Good."

"Helen!"

"I'm sorry, Annie. I know you're too involved to see it, but this Superman–Clark Kent thing seems studied to me. And isn't it a coincidence that all these spooky things start happening to you right after you start seeing him?"

Helen had a point, one Annie didn't want to dwell on too closely.

"What about it, Nick?" she asked, hoping for his support despite the mob connection he'd managed to come up with—to her knowledge, a connection he hadn't shared with anyone but her. "Do you agree with Helen?"

Nick studied the contents of his cup. "I think you ought to be careful, that's all."

Careful how? Annie wondered. By looking over her shoulder everywhere she went? She was already doing that. Surely he didn't think she shouldn't be seeing Nate? He hadn't backed up Helen, at least not directly.

Knowing she should call Nate and talk to him about the situation, Annie left for the shop with the intention of doing so. But Gloria was already there. And while her personal business should remain personal, Annie feared that she might not be the only one in some kind of danger. This had started with the business itself, she thought, and for all she knew, Gloria could be next.

As Annie told her about the phone call, Gloria's eyes went round. But before the name *Julio* could fly from her lips, Annie told her about the police report as well.

"It's that no-*cajones* Clive Hardy! I told you to let me take care of him!"

"The police will take care of him, if he's the one."

Gloria pursed her lips. "Mmm-hmm."

"Don't go getting any ideas now. But keep an eye out for him. And Burdock and Zavadinski. Let me know if you spot any one of them around the building today."

Though the security guard had every right to be there, unless he was fired, of course. Annie couldn't exactly alert the authorities that he was hanging around the building when that's exactly what he was supposed to do.

Reminded of Nate, she set out to make that call. There was no answer—not at his home, not on his private office line. She thought to call the general number, but she really didn't want to leave a message with his assistant any more than she wanted to leave a recorded one.

Odd that he hadn't called her. Surely the police had contacted him by now.

An onslaught of lunchtime customers kept her from dwelling on the matter. Later that afternoon, however, when she got back into her office and unsuccessfully tried to reach him again, she started to worry.

Was Nate angry with her for not getting in touch with him sooner? Or was he avoiding her for some other reason?

No, she wouldn't allow herself to suspect him.

She attacked the pile of mail. Started sorting the bills from the bulk mail…until a familiar-looking envelope, one without postage, stared up at her.

Hands trembling, she opened it.

Dear Annie,
How many people know the real you? How many people do you want to?

We all walk around wearing one face, hiding another. Do you ever get tired of playing the game?

When I look at you, I see you for what you are. Do you see me at all?

An Admirer

She couldn't believe it—this on the heels of the recording. Helen had been right about one thing: her secret admirer was a weirdo.

And so was she for having once seen the letters as playful and sexy.

How wrong could one woman be?

ANNIE SPENT the latter part of the afternoon shopping for supplies. After receiving the latest missive, she'd gotten an idea for the display window.

And then, figuring she would be working late into the night, she had an early dinner at a local eatery—a big dinner since she'd skipped both breakfast and lunch. While doing so, she sketched out her ideas.

She headed back for the shop just before closing time.

"Any calls?" she asked Gloria, who was getting ready to leave.

"Not a one."

No Nate. Her chest tightened.

"All right, then," she muttered, setting down her bags near the window.

Standing at the front door, Gloria crossed her arms

and tapped her foot. "You ain't planning on staying here alone."

"Better here than home."

"Then I'll just have to stay with you."

"No, you won't. I'm fine. And I need to concentrate."

"Annie, I don't like this."

"Well, I don't, either," Annie admitted. "I don't like someone stalking me. I don't like being afraid. I don't like looking over my shoulder every minute. But these are the facts of life at the moment, and I will survive it!" She'd never seen Gloria gape at her in such surprise before. "I appreciate your concern and your loyalty, but this is something I have to handle on my own."

Muttering something in Spanish under her breath, Gloria opened the door and started to leave. Then she stopped herself and wagged her finger at Annie.

"Don't you go getting yourself into no terrible trouble, or I ain't never gonna forgive you. And if you want a place to stay tonight that isn't yours, you know my number."

"Gloria, you mean a lot to me, too."

"Humph. Then lock this door behind me."

Annie did as she was ordered and waved goodbye to her worried employee through the glass. Then she turned and went straight to the back door, making sure it was locked, as well.

She'd called the authorities, for all the good it had done her. They'd been honest with her. They would talk to people, but unless there was an actual threat....

In the meantime, she wasn't going to give up her

freedom—always having to be protected by one of her friends, never being alone or going about business as usual. She had a life and she was going to live it.

Trying to put her stalker out of mind, she got down to work on her new display, one meant to explore everyone's notion of identity.

On a large piece of board that would serve as a backdrop, she sketched in the outline of Chicago as seen from the lake—myriad skyscrapers in comic-book style. By the time she was satisfied with the results, several hours had passed. Midnight had come and gone without her realizing it.

Traffic along the street was minimal. Still, the possibility of an occasional passerby prompted her to turn off the store lights. Annie wanted total privacy. A surprise for the morning commuters who would stop and, hopefully, be intrigued and amused.

She worked in the window itself, by moonlight and the blue-green cast of the streetlamps. Every so often she would stare out through the gauzy, makeshift curtain, wondering if anyone was staring back. Not that anyone could see her without a light in the display area itself. Not unless the person came right up to the glass.

After setting the backdrop in place, she dressed the female mannequin and draped her across a settee dragged out from one of the dressing rooms. Finally Annie got to the male mannequin. She had barely finished dressing and posing it when she realized she wasn't alone.

Starting, she whipped around to find Nate watching her from the darkened center of the store. He was leaning against a support pillar, arms crossed over his chest.

Her heart thumped as she looked him over. He wasn't smiling, and his stance suggested that he was majorly upset.

"How long have you been watching me?" she whispered, curling her hands into fists so they wouldn't shake.

A familiar question. Nate always seemed to be trying to get under her skin.

"Not long."

"How did you get in?" she demanded. "And don't try to tell me I left the back door open again, because I checked it after Gloria left."

"I used my passkey."

As he had the night of the gallery opening? Had he lied then? she wondered.

He was angry. She could see it in the taut line of his body as he moved toward her, recognized it in the timbre of his voice. Not that he'd raised it. But he couldn't hide what he was feeling. Not from her.

A frisson of unease slid up her spine, while other, more enticing sensations attacked her tender parts. She was torn between fear and desire.

And then Nate took one last threatening step closer and demanded, "Why did you keep that call you got last night to yourself, Annie? Why send a couple of cops after me?"

"I'm sorry." Getting control of herself, at least for the moment, she said, "I did try to call you."

"Not hard enough."

"You didn't answer!" She couldn't help but be on

the defensive. "You had enough time to get home. More than enough time! So where were you?"

"Here, as a matter of fact."

"In my shop?" She looked around wildly, as though she could see signs of trespassing that she'd missed earlier.

"The janitor's closet. I wanted to know what happened that you got locked in."

"Well?"

"The locked jammed. It was as simple as that. I fixed it and set the door back on its hinges."

Annie supposed he had—not that she'd thought to check the door today. But she believed he'd fixed it. He was a hands-on kind of landlord.

Again he asked, "So why didn't you keep calling until you reached me?"

"I did try today, both at your home and on your private line at the office. You didn't answer."

"You couldn't leave me a message?"

"I don't usually leave messages about my sex life."

Again she felt threatened as Nate roughly said, "It's not just sex between us, Annie! And I'm not just anyone!"

"Then who are you?" The words slipped out too fast to stop them.

"Is that it?" He sounded incredulous. "You didn't make the effort to let me know what was going on because you don't know who I am?" He moved into her comfort zone, backing her against a pillar. "I know who you are, Annie. Why don't you know me?"

When I look at you, I see you for what you are, the latest missive had said. *Do you see me at all?* Trepidation dried up her mouth and she stood there mute, her pulse jagging through her. *Could it be…?*

"Don't you find it odd that you believe what's inside is so important that you can't actually see me as a whole person?" Nate asked. "Why is that, I wonder?"

"I don't know what—"

"Don't deny it. What's so wrong with Nathaniel that you can't see past the suit to who I really am? All of me. Nathaniel and Nate together. We're one and the same person, Annie. Just as the hidden woman behind this disguise of yours is the real you." He indicated her usual nondescript outfit of the day. "Everyone is more than one person. So why do I have to play dress-up for you? Why do I have to be Nate for you to want to be with me?"

"I don't know," she hedged, then lightly added, "That seductive bad-boy image would probably appeal to any woman."

"But you're not just any woman. Not to me."

Then he looked past her to the display.

Wearing romantic lounge wear, the female mannequin was in a pose of distress, looking over her shoulder, as if she feared something or someone behind her. Her face was covered by a fancy feathered and sequined mask to give her an added air of mystery. Turned toward her but at a slight distance, the male mannequin was dressed in a suit with hat and glasses, but was pulling at his tie, as if to remove it.

A bit of blue material showed above the pristine white shirt.

She meant for his disguise to be peeled back a layer at a time, a day at a time. And she planned to change the lounge wear to display the new line, while keeping the same mask on the mannequin.

Nate stepped into the shop window, away from her. He tugged down the male mannequin's tie and opened the shirt, then took a good look at the garment beneath the business gear. When he cursed under his breath, Annie swallowed hard. Of course he recognized the Superman costume.

"Is everything a game to you?" Her Superman–Clark Kent lover sounded outraged.

"I thought that was your specialty." She licked her lips, but her mouth was dry. "Dangerous games."

"Maybe I really *am* dangerous, Annie." His voice went low. "Maybe you recognize that and that's what *really* turns you on about me."

Her heart thudded, but she protested, "No." She might be afraid, but not because she feared he would hurt her physically. "I don't believe that."

Their relationship was all pretend. All fantasy. *That's* what turned her on.

Reality romance was a big washout as far as she was concerned.

"Then what is it?" His gaze ground into her. "What do you have against expensive suits? Or should I say against the men who wear them?"

He'd figured it out sort of. She guessed it wouldn't hurt to tell him the rest. "Alan Cooper, law student, the only other guy I ever fell for."

"Why? What did he do to you?"

His intensity forced her to relive that humiliating, world-shattering moment.

"After I, uh, slept with him, I learned that he'd had a bet with his fraternity brothers. He had to sleep with the woman on campus most unlikely to lose her virginity, and make her fall in love with him. Alan had me seeing stars and dancing on air and dreaming of a shared future, while he was laughing at me with his friends. I heard him," she admitted, remembering as if it had happened yesterday rather than years ago.

"So the bastard broke your heart and I remind you of him?"

Unable to look at Nate directly, she admitted, "Nathaniel does sometimes."

"So he scares you?"

Remembering Nick had said the very same thing, she shrugged her shoulders. "Maybe."

"Then you're in love with him? Me? Us?"

"I never said that."

"Then say it, Annie." Again, he backed her up against the support pillar at the edge of the display. "What are you waiting for?"

Though her body sang with her response, she shook her head. Nick had been right about her fears, after all. Good old Nick. The words were there, but she couldn't do it. She never wanted to say them again.

And if he'd been right about one thing…

"Nate, tell me you had nothing to do with that tape."

"I had nothing to do with that tape."

He said it as if by rote, as if to placate her. Could

she believe him? She wanted to...but what if this were the ultimate game and he was determined to win? What if Helen had been right about Nate all along?

"How far would you go?" she asked.

"For you?"

"To get what you want from me."

"As far as I have to. Now it's your turn to be honest. How do you feel about me, Annie?"

She couldn't say it. Couldn't mouth the words more dangerous than anything that had happened to her. And why should she? He hadn't spoken of loving her, just about wanting her, like a possession.

What if this *were* a game to him? Was he any different from Alan Cooper? He would go as far as he had to, he'd said. Would he cheat? Would he send notes, take photographs, tape their lovemaking?

To what end? To excite her? To make her turn to him? Trust him with her life?

As if he knew exactly what it would take to get what he wanted, Nate dipped his head and covered her mouth with his, covered her body with his. He pressed up against her and tried to seduce the truth from her. And though her mind screamed at her to resist, her body was weak. Instantly on fire, she moaned and wrapped her arms around his neck. This was so easy for him. For him, she was so very easy.

"You said, 'The only *other* guy I ever fell for.' Did you fall for me? Say it, Annie," he murmured against her mouth. "Don't be afraid."

What was wrong with her? Why couldn't she stop him? Stop herself? Why couldn't she take a time-out until her stalker was caught and she could be absolutely sure?

"I—I want..."

"What?"

She tried to say the things she should, the things that would keep her safe, but the words wouldn't come. The only thing she could say was the truth.

"You. I want you."

13

“YOU HAVE ME, sweetheart,” Nate murmured against her mouth. “Any day, anytime.”

He rocked his hips into her. He was as ready as she was. But as much as she wanted to, he supposed she wouldn't...not here, not now...

Or would she?

Without letting go of her, without stopping the kiss, Nate turned Annie and moved her back against the settee, propelling her over the arm, while shoving the hapless mannequin to the floor. In the process, he knocked over several bottles of massage oil she'd set there as part of the display.

Ineffectually pushing at his chest, she complained, “Someone will see.”

“No one will care.”

As he tugged at the string that tightened her trousers around her waist, she cried out, “Nate!”

“That's it. Say my name. I like that little catch in your voice. It turns me on.”

She licked her lips, and he knew he had her then. All of her. No matter that she wouldn't say the words he wanted to hear. She was showing him, he thought. She was letting him lead her wherever he would take her. His plan had worked. Annie Wilder was his.

A fast glance at the street assured Nate that no one

was around to see. But she knew as well as he did that there was always the potential for discovery. Wasn't that part of the thrill for her?

He already had the trousers and her panties half off when he felt her pulse quicken as it always did when he convinced her to take chances. Wondering if they were ever destined to make love in a more conventional manner, he let the thought slide away as he slipped a finger deep inside her.

"You're so wet for me," he murmured, feeling his erection grow harder at the discovery.

He released himself from his jeans and heard her quick intake of breath. Hot and wet and panting, she was ready for him. By the time he leaned over her, she was pulling at him too, obviously eager for him to ride her.

He would give her everything she wanted and more, Nate vowed. He was crazy for her and would do anything to please her, to keep her tied to him, perhaps forever. He couldn't imagine life without her anymore.

The tear of packaging and the snap of latex as he put on a condom seemed to echo off the glass. With her gaze focused on his face, Annie raised her hips and pulled at him until he slid partially into her.

Still on his feet, he balanced himself by bracing both hands against the settee. She snaked her legs up around his waist and rocked against him.

"Not so fast—"

"Yes, fast," she insisted. "Hard, too. And deep."

Her talking—finally doing what he'd been urging her to do all week—nearly set Nate off. He shoved hard and went deep over and over, faster and faster.

She arched her back and managed to pull his head down so she could kiss him and thrust her tongue in his mouth in the same rhythm. Then, when the tension had built in him to a crisis point, she sucked his upper lip and nipped at it.

He cried out and this time came without her, but Annie took every inch of him until he was spent.

When he sagged against her, she wiggled upward, using her feet against the settee edge for leverage. His head landed on her breast. A tantalizing bite through her clothing made her moan for more. She took a quick look out the window, and the next thing he knew, she'd removed her top and bra. He obliged her by tonguing one nipple, while rubbing the other between thumb and forefinger, pulling from her a series of sounds, both of pleasure and frustration.

He suspected she anticipated they would have sex again, right now, but he wasn't really Superman.

Or was he? he wondered as she slid a hand down between them, and finding him nestled against her leg, removed the spent condom. He was already responding. Her touching him, cajoling him with her fingertips and nails, did wonders to restore his confidence.

"A man of steel," she murmured with a sigh as she coaxed his flesh back into full erection.

JUST TO BE SURE they had no audience, Annie took a fast look-see through the shrouded display window as she reached down for a bottle of massage oil, then quickly opened it and dripped some on one palm.

The street was dark and deserted, with not even a moving car in sight. Relieved, she rubbed her palms together until the fragrant scent of freesia drifted up to tantalize her nose. Then she slipped her oiled hands between them, down along Nate's belly, over his penis, under his scrotum. Sliding back along his length, she alternately smoothed his skin and bit into him with the tips of her nails as further incentive. With all of this going on in a store window, the possibility of discovery was there—she knew that—but she couldn't stop herself, not now, not when she had Nate right in the palm of her hand.

"Condom?" she whispered.

He reached down to the floor and seconds later produced the packet with a flourish. "Always prepared," he murmured, ripping it open.

"The Boy Scout motto?"

Continuing to stroke his flesh with oiled hands, she watched him expertly roll on the condom, noting that the head was so engorged it was nearly purple. She closed her eyes a second and imagined come shooting from the cleft. A rush of wet warmth lubricated her even as she felt him lean forward so that very tip pressed against her labia.

"I was never a Boy Scout," he admitted as he parted her with a thrust.

He then began to move with tantalizing slowness, and she couldn't make him hurry again. Couldn't make him go deep enough or fast enough, no matter how she urged him. Another few drops of oil gave her fingers a slippery playground to draw designs on his back and along his sides. He groaned but couldn't be coaxed to move faster. Sweat beaded her body and she tried losing herself anyway, tried reaching for something that wouldn't come.

He was teasing her. Bringing her to the edge, then pulling back. She fairly vibrated inside. Pulsed. Needed. She was ready—more than ready—but still he wouldn't give her that explosive release.

"Tell me what you want me to do to you," he murmured into her ear.

Letting go of the last of her inhibitions, she pleaded, "Make love to me like you mean it!"

"I mean it," he told her, his voice barely controlled. "Convince me that *you* do."

She tried to make him lose himself, so she could do the same. But no matter how she stroked him, how she shifted positions to excite him, he seemed impervious.

Thinking of something that might do the trick, she pushed him away slightly and, with another drip from the oil bottle, started touching *herself*—her breasts first, so that he would see her and be totally aware of her actions. The oil spreading over her skin made a slight sucking sound under her hands. Letting her eyes flutter closed, she squeezed her nipples and moaned.

When he groaned in response, she knew that finally she had him.

She slid a hand down between them and found her clit. Rubbing her forefinger against it, she moaned again and arched her back so that she pressed seductively against him.

"Annie!" Nate groaned, shoving in deep and trapping her hand between them.

Taking her mouth, he plunged his tongue inside. Then he worked her with matching rhythms, in and out, in and out, until she sparked inside and went off like a cherry bomb—intensely enough and loudly enough for the sound to echo around the display area.

The sensation seemed to stretch on forever, and when she was finally spent, Annie realized that Nate had collapsed with her. She held on tightly. She wasn't going to let the feeling go, not now, not when she felt this perfect happiness. Nothing mattered but being with Nate, being one with him, so that she no longer knew where he left off and she began.

They were so good together. It was as if he knew her every need and did his best to fulfill her every fantasy, at least at times like this. Times when logic didn't matter. Times when the idea of danger was more exciting than frightening.

Her reality had been too conservative for far too long. This fantasy-come-true was what she wanted. *He* was what she wanted.

Whoever he was.

For she still didn't know him. Didn't know if he was really Nate or Nathaniel, or both, as he declared. She only knew that when she was with him like this, she felt fulfilled as never before. Happy. Sated with sex and safe in his arms.

He managed to wedge a hip next to her and pull her close, wrapped in his arms. One leg straddled hers protectively. He felt so good.... This felt so good she never wanted to move.

At least not until the buzz wore off and doubts began to creep back in. Doubts she tried to ignore.

"Maybe we ought to get dressed," she said.

"A little longer," he argued, obviously not ready to let her go.

"What if someone gets close to the window and sees?"

Yet another glance at the street assured Annie that it was still empty of pedestrians, with only a stray taxi moving through the intersection.

Nate's responding laughter brushed against her insides. He'd never sounded happier. "A little late to worry about that, isn't it?" he asked, lazily trailing a finger through a puddle of oil on her breast as though he wanted to make love again.

Her nipple tightened, as did her insides, and Annie feared that if he pressed her, she would be putty in his hands.

Yet he made no other move, just cupped her breast gently and seemed content to lie there, precariously balanced behind her on the settee. That he just wanted to be with her warmed her inside. And so she leaned back against him, let herself go. For a moment let herself think of deeper emotions than those comfortable to admit.

Love... Did she?

She barely thought it, and didn't have time to explore the question before her eyes grew heavy and she dozed a bit, warm and safe in the shelter of his body.

Suddenly, it seemed, he lifted his weight off her, and she would have fallen to the display floor if he hadn't steadied her. "C'mon, Sleeping Beauty, time to get up, or my back will never be the same."

With his help, she rose from the settee and, scooping up her clothes, left the display area. Then, in the dimness of the store, she dressed with his uninvited help. His touch rekindled banked fires. But he didn't go further.

Why? Because there was no challenge? How much more dangerous could he make things? she wondered. What was left?

"When was the last time you, uh, made it in a bed?" she asked, then swiftly changed her mind. "No, don't answer that. I really don't want to know when. But you have used a bed before, right?"

"On occasion. Want to try mine?" A slow grin captured his mouth and he captured her, snaking his arms around her waist and pulling her tight against him. "We can be at my place in five minutes."

She groaned. "You don't want me to be able to walk tomorrow."

"If I could get away with it, I would keep you chained to my bed forever."

She pushed back so that she could see his face through the shadows. "You're kidding, right?"

"What do you think?"

She tried to read him, but couldn't. "Sometimes it's hard to know with you."

"That's because you don't trust me."

"Of course I do. What do you call what we just did?"

"You trust Nate, maybe, but not me."

"You are Nate." Suddenly perturbed, she wiggled out of his arms and tried to straighten her hair.

"And I'm Nathaniel. And you still have a problem with that."

Annie couldn't deny it, but she didn't want to get into it, didn't want to spoil the moment, so she said nothing. But he, it seemed, had no such problem.

"You're mine, Annie, not just Nate's." He smoothed stray hair from her cheek. "It's time you come to terms with that fact."

Annie ducked away from him. "Maybe I don't want to be yours," she argued. "Not Nate's, either. Maybe I want to belong to myself."

"Sounds like a lonely road to me. And a safe one."

"Nothing wrong with safe." Better than throwing her heart out, only to have it shredded.

"Of course there is. It's not you. You're the one who likes dangerous games, remember." He trailed his hand down her throat. "You're the one who likes to take chances. So why not take a chance with me? I mean, all of me."

"I have been taking chances."

"Not the kind that count."

"Don't push, Nate."

"Don't confuse me with Alan Cooper."

Any residual warmth she'd been feeling from their lovemaking dissolved at the reminder of the man who'd made such a fool of her.

"I need to get home!" Annie snapped.

"I think we need to talk this out."

"I am talked out. If you really knew me the way you say you do, you would have figured that out."

His expression drained to neutral and he took a step back and stared as if he were really seeing her for the first time.

"You're not ever going to give me a break, are you?" he asked.

She couldn't meet his gaze, so she stared at his lips—too dangerous. At the cleft in his chin. "I've given you more than you know."

Silence stretched between them for an interminable moment before he said, "Lock up and I'll take you home."

"I know the way." And before he could object, tell her it wasn't safe, she added, "I can give a taxi driver directions, thanks."

He went still and his expression closed, and for a moment, Annie saw the stranger again. The one who was neither Nate nor Nathaniel. The one who made her mouth go dry and her breath catch in her throat.

"If you do this, Annie, you'll regret it."

"What? Not let you take me home?"

He didn't answer, merely shook his head and backed off. Annie hugged herself and watched him leave by the back door, the way he'd come in, without so much as another glance her way.

What had he meant by regret? Somehow, she didn't think it was the going home issue. She supposed it was a matter of trust, of her not accepting all sides of him.

Would she regret it?

She would if he tired of her, tired of the game he thought she was playing with him, when in fact she wasn't playing at all. Not about this. She was protecting herself. And that was something that needed no apology, she decided.

Her anger on simmer, she called the cab company and was told a taxi would be at her door in a matter of minutes.

Straightening the display window and gathering her things, she locked up the shop. Only after waiting outside for several minutes did she begin to wonder if she'd made a mistake, and if someone were watching her again.

Nate? Or someone more dangerous?

Though she saw no one, her unease grew and multiplied. It was the circumstances, she told herself. Until her stalker was identified and put out of commission, she would be looking over her shoulder wherever she was. She was about to go back inside when a taxi finally flew through the intersection and slid to a stop at the curb.

Climbing inside, she glanced out the back window at the naked street as they pulled away and sped toward her place.

Only her imagination…

If only that self-assurance would quiet her nerves!

Unlike the cabbie the other night, who had been concerned enough to watch her get into her place safely, this one sped away the moment she got out of the vehicle and slammed the door.

And she was left in the dark, with the too-familiar feeling of personal invasion.

After fumbling with the keys long enough to stretch her nerves taut, she got the front door open and shot inside. Before she could finish bolting it behind her, Rock was twirling around her ankles.

"Hey, sweet boy," she murmured, lifting him into her arms, once more remembering the comment about his being the male in her life. Maybe he was, she decided as she marched the cat over to his food bowl.

Why did Nate have to be so difficult? Why couldn't he understand where she was coming from? What was wrong with having a good time together, fulfilling her fantasies and leaving reality to others?

"Here you go," she murmured to Rock as she emptied a can of tuna into his dish. He waited for her to pet him and then he hunkered down and started to eat.

Nearly any guy would kill to have such a smooth setup—all the sex he wanted and no sticky commitment.

Nate wasn't most guys, a little voice argued. She wouldn't want him if he was. Therein lay her quandary, because it was Nate she wanted and only Nate. And yet...

She wasn't actually averse to commitment, either, Annie thought as she headed for the shower. Just gun-shy. She didn't want to believe in something that wasn't about to happen. Her giving Nathaniel a break didn't mean that she'd have nirvana forever as a result. What if, once he had her—Nathaniel as well as Nate—he walked away? Annie didn't know if it was a risk she was willing to take.

Showered and shampooed and feeling a little better a quarter of an hour later, she pulled on a cotton nightshirt and set out for bed. Rock hopped up beside her, then walked around to her pillow, where he wrapped himself around her head, pressed his paws into her scalp and snorted into her still-damp hair.

Annie laughed, patted him and cooed to him until he settled down to sleep.

Now thoughts and images of her and Nate together whirled in her mind, keeping her from falling asleep. She needed to do something physical, to wear off this sex-induced residual energy.

Might as well do something useful, she thought, getting up carefully so as not to disturb the cat.

A few minutes later, she was in the room where she and Nate had been intimate the other night. Thinking about the phone call and the tape, she hesitated in the doorway. But she'd already gone through the room, searching for a hidden microphone that didn't exist. No doubt the pervert had done as the police suggested and had taped them from outside.

Still, she approached her task with a sense of unease. She started going through boxes, looking for things she could use to make her place feel more like home. Finding those frames again reminded her of the other night. Feeling a little tense, she was just setting them to one side when a sudden noise behind her made her start and whip around.

The cat had come to supervise.

"Oh, it's only you." Her heart sank back down out of her throat and her pulse settled as Rock investigated an open box. "Want to help me pick out some good stuff? Meow if you see something you like."

A small lamp with a glass bead shade appealed to her. She plugged it in the wall outlet and was delighted to find it still worked. Perfect for her bedside.

She continued searching and sorting. Things she could use in her window displays went in one pile, things to bring downstairs to cheer up the place in another. The cat sat and watched her every movement with interest.

In the middle of combing through a box of crochet-trimmed hankies and doilies, Annie found her mind wandering back to her argument with Nate. How had that happened so quickly after they'd shared themselves with each other? she wondered. And what would he do to make her sorry?

"You definitely are the most *reasonable* male in my life," she told Rock.

At the sound of her voice, the cat started to come to her, then stopped. Eyes wide on something behind her, back arched, he growled deep in his throat.

"Rock, honey, what—?"

Before she could ask him what was wrong—if he saw another rat or something—the cat zoomed past her and through the partially open door.

Spooked, her pulse fluttering as she remembered the other times the cat had growled like that—not all having to do with rodents—Annie decided to go back downstairs herself. Sorting estate treasures could wait. She set the box away from her and shot to her feet. But before she could leave the room, the door slammed with a loud *bam!* as if closed by an invisible hand.

Annie froze and stared at the wooden panel. "Is someone there?" she blurted out, before realizing the ridiculousness of asking. If someone had broken into the place, he certainly wouldn't be so civilized as to answer.

Her stalker?

Her pulse pounded in dread even as she tried to convince herself that a draft had shut the door. Maybe no one was there. After all, how would he have gotten in? Crossing to the door, she tried to turn the knob, but just as in the janitor's closet, she was locked in from the outside.

Nate had assured her the lock had simply jammed, but it was too much to believe that could happen twice in as many days. Someone had purposely jammed them both.

Heart in her throat, she banged on the door. "Open up, coward!" she yelled. "Open up and face me, if you're man enough!"

In answer, the lights went out.

Annie tried not to hyperventilate as she felt her way to the small lamp she'd found and flipped the switch. Nothing! The power had been cut. If she'd been frightened in the janitor's closet, she was terrified now.

Locked in a room without electricity…without an escape hatch…without a weapon!

She couldn't even defend herself, Annie realized. Not that someone was actually trying to hurt her. More like playing a sick game with her.

A game?

She shook her head and tried to clear it of all but positive thoughts, her only regret being that she'd chased off Nate when he could be here with her now.

The room did have windows. She ran to one that was open, slid it all the way up the track. She didn't worry about locking the second-floor windows because they were so high that she figured no one could get to them without a ladder.

A gust of wind shot through the opening, pebbling her skin. She looked down at the ground, and found the drop was too far for her comfort zone—a leg breaker if she ever saw one. And she'd never been particularly athletic.

Now what?

Leaning out of the window, she saw that a shallow, decorative cement ledge several inches wide ran around the brick building, along the upper floor. Could she make it to a window in the other second-floor room and back inside? Hopefully, she'd left that one unlocked, as well. Her stomach knotted and she swallowed hard. She didn't like heights!

But she could do this, she told herself. As long as she didn't make the mistake of looking down, she could do it. Besides, what choice did she have? Her stalker could close in on her at any moment.

With trepidation, she climbed out of the window and felt for the ledge with her bare foot. Her stomach roiling, threatening to empty, she set her other foot down. She took a big breath and concentrated on the end goal. Flattening her back against the building, she inched to her left. Her toes curled along the edge with each step.

The night was quiet, eerily so. Annie strained to hear anything coming from within the building—like the stalker going nuts because he'd discovered she wasn't locked in that room—but the only sound was the rustle of leaves when the wind picked up.

The moon slid in and out of cloud banks, but as she crept along the side of the building, her eyes adjusted and she was able to pick out details around her…like the conduit bringing electricity to the second floor.

With one careful motion, she grabbed on to it and swung herself around, facing the other window. Her stomach rocked but quickly settled. Now if only the damn thing would open, she thought, using the heel of one hand to shove up the sash.

It did!

"Thank you!" she whispered into the night.

If she could enter the room undiscovered, she could slip down the stairs and out the door….

Carefully, she climbed over the sill, then waited for a moment while her pulse steadied. No sound cut through the stillness, so she groped along the wall to the door. The knob turned and a taste of victory flushed through her.

Ear to the thick wood, she listened intently, but picked up no sound on the other side. Taking a deep breath for courage, she inched the door open just enough to slip out and down the hall to the staircase. She moved silently, her bare feet skimming the wood floor. Not daring to breathe too deeply, she could only hope that her stalker remained unaware of her escape attempt.

Counting steps until she got to the bottom, she studied the area around her, still dark but for the hint of moonlight coming from the high windows. No ominous shadows separated from the rest. Nothing moved.

She pictured herself escaping—crossing the entryway, unlocking the door and opening it, fleeing into the night. She wouldn't be able to take Rock with her, but prayed the cat would stay hidden and safe until she could call for help.

It was time.

Without a whisper of sound she made it to the door and felt for the locks. But before her trembling fingers could get the dead bolt open, her arm was caught in a fierce grip.

Annie screamed and lashed out, trying to pull away, but her attacker was stronger than she and whipped her away from the door and into her living quarters.

"What do you want? Who are you? Why can't you just let me be?"

"I'm your worst fantasy, Annie," came whispered words that nearly sent her into shock.

"Who—?"

Again he whipped her around and pushed her back, and she felt something solid behind her knees before she fell backward onto her bed.

"No!" she screamed, thrashing with her free arm, hitting him with a closed fist, trying to roll as she felt him press down on her.

Her small size put her at a disadvantage. He grabbed her other wrist and easily pinned both hands above her head. Then he began to touch her, to seek a way under her nightgown. She bucked and tried to knee him, but she was already exhausted and, despite the adrenaline rush, couldn't free herself.

Her skin crawled where he touched it and she realized that if she didn't think of something, she would be another statistic.

"Stop!" she screamed at him. "What kind of a man are you that you have to force a woman?"

He whispered, "What kind of a woman gets off on it?"

Adrenaline shot through her and she used it to roll to one hip, unseating him. Off balance, he loosened his grip, and she freed a hand. And when he tried to recapture it, she caught one of his fingers and bent it back hard enough to make him grunt.

"Bitch!"

From somewhere nearby, she heard Rock hiss, then yowl. And then the cat sprang onto the bed and ran over her attacker's back.

"Shit!" the man yelped, letting go of Annie long enough that she rolled out from under him and ran for the door. She heard the stalker rush after her, trip and fall and curse again.

Then she was out the door, running for all she was worth, ignoring the stones and other debris that bruised her feet. All she could think about was getting to Nate. But first she had to hide.

She ducked into a nearby alley, praying her stalker hadn't seen which way she'd gone, and looked around wildly for cover. The garbage cans! She hunkered down behind one of the black resin units. On wheels, it would serve as a battering ram in case he caught up to her. In the meantime, she breathed deeply and calmed herself with thoughts of Nate and being safe in his arms. She replayed the image over and over, used it to clear her head.

Five minutes passed with no sounds indicating that anyone was after her.

Was her stalker still there? Inside her place? Waiting for her to be foolish enough to return?

Ten minutes.

Annie stood and tested her limbs. Everything was in working order. Nothing felt too abused but her bare feet. She crept back to the mouth of the alley to peek out at her street. No lights were on in her building. No one was moving around.

What to do? Should she go to some stranger's house and pound at the door in the middle of the night? That would only draw attention to herself, perhaps unwanted attention.

Annie started walking down the street, thinking she would somehow get to Nate's place. He would keep her safe. He would take her in his arms and then everything would be all right.

As she rounded a corner, she saw a vehicle coming and recognized the shape of lights atop it, the blue-and-white paint of a Chicago squad car.

Reeling with relief, she stood in the street and flagged down the cops on the beat.

14

THE SMELL OF FOOD tantalizing her nostrils pulled Annie up out of a deep sleep. At first she was disoriented. Strange bed. Strange room. And then she remembered Nate.

Still dressed, she rose and used his bathroom to freshen up before going downstairs. The kitchen, she noted as she entered, was perfection in boring maple and granite.

"I must be dreaming," she said, sniffing the mouthwatering aroma and rubbing her eyes. "A man making me breakfast."

"Actually, I had breakfast delivered."

She focused on Nate working at the kitchen counter and thought she could get used to waking up to the sight every morning. "Still, the last time that happened was...well, never."

"Then I'm a first."

"In more ways than one," she admitted as he invited her to sit at the table he'd set for two. Though he'd ordered out, he'd put the food on real plates. "How did I not hear the delivery person?"

"I waited at the door and took it from him before he could get to the buzzer."

She took a taste of food and another and another. Watching her intently, Nate ate at a slower pace.

Then she broke the silence. "Nate, thanks. Really."

"It's just breakfast."

"No, not that. Well, that, too. I mean for being there—here—when I needed you."

"I just wish I hadn't let you talk me out of taking you home last night. Then you never would have been attacked."

Hunkered behind a garbage can, she'd wished the same thing. "My fault. I was freaking for nothing. All I did was bring bad luck down on myself."

"About that. The bastard is still running free. He could come back. I think you should move into my place, at least until the police nab him."

The food she was swallowing caught in her throat. She washed it down with a big gulp of coffee. Though she liked seeing Nate's domestic side, she couldn't make that big a leap in commitment. Yet he was right that she might not be safe at home for the moment.

"Helen wouldn't mind a temporary roomie, I'm sure," she mumbled.

"So you won't consider staying here at my place."

Nathaniel's place, she thought, though she didn't say it. "I don't know you well enough to move in with you."

"You know me well enough to have sex with me," he countered. Frowning, he rose from the table. "I don't believe this."

"Nate, please..."

"Please what? Don't be yourself, Nate? Play to my fantasies, Nate, and then disappear so I don't have to think of you as a real person? Which fantasy does this whole scenario fit into?"

I'm your worst fantasy....

Annie shoved the food away from her and began to shake.

And Nate was at her side in a minute. "I'm sorry, okay? I didn't mean to upset you again." He took her in his arms and held her close, as though he might never let her go. After a moment he said, "Call Helen and set it up. I'll take you home to pack a bag and then deliver you to her place. And the cat, if you can find him."

Rock had been hiding again. Her furry hero had come out to see for himself that she was all right and then had slunk away again.

"For all I know, he's still hiding under the bed." Realizing Nate was nearly as upset as she, Annie nodded. "All right. It's a plan."

The first thing she wanted to do after calling a too-quiet, too-calm Helen, was take a shower, something she hadn't bothered with after the police left. She hadn't wanted to let go of Nate even for a few minutes.

But in the clear light of day, she felt stronger, angrier. And while she washed away the remnants of last night's terror, she tried to figure out how best to protect herself until the police arrested someone.

A vial of pepper spray was definitely in order. And maybe one of those personal alarms, noisier than a car alarm. And an attack dog...or maybe not. Rock had done her proud. He was a real attack cat, she thought with a wry smile as she remembered him growling so fiercely.

That growl...she'd only heard him so upset those few times. The night she'd gotten the first letter and had called Nate, who'd then discovered the rat. The night of Helen's birthday celebration. The day Annie had gotten the photographs. And last night.

Odd. And odd that Rock wouldn't come out from under the bed for her when they got back to her place. With Nate by her side all the way, she checked and found him huddled in the middle.

"Hey, sweetheart, come on out." But her wheedling got her nowhere.

"He'll calm down eventually and come out to eat and use his litter," Nate said. "We'll just make sure he has what he needs."

"I hate leaving him here all alone, though. What if the stalker comes back and hurts him? I don't even know how the creep got into the place. No signs of a break-in. The police figured I left a door or lower window open, but I swear I didn't. And he couldn't have gotten in through one of the second-story windows without a ladder. No sign of that, either."

"Maybe he had a key."

"That's impossible. I don't give out keys." *At least not to nonexistent boyfriends.*

"No one has a spare?"

"No one but Helen. And Nick would have access to it, since he knows where they're kept."

Nate digested that. "Well, we should change the locks, anyway."

We?

"And if you'll let me," he added, "I'll get my security guy in here to install a system."

"I don't know—"

"Well, you should! You've been attacked here in more ways than one. You need to let me do this for you, Annie, unless you plan on moving in with Helen permanently."

"No, this is my home!"

"So let me make it safe."

In the end she caved in, because she knew he was right.

A quarter of an hour later, he walked her to Helen's door, brushed her lips with his and left her with the promise that he would see her later. And that he would see to her cat, who'd refused to come out of hiding no matter what she'd done to lure him into the open.

Thankfully, Helen didn't lecture her the way Annie thought she might. She kept cool, even in the face of Annie's insistance about going to work as usual.

"So, will there be an actual investigation now that you've been attacked?" Helen asked, as they got into her old Jaguar, a leftover from her dot.com salad days.

"They took fingerprints."

"What if the stalker has never been arrested?"

Annie relaxed against the leather seat, the smell of which reminded her of Nate when he was dressed for a wild ride on the Harley. "Then he'll be harder to find."

"What aren't you telling me?"

"That I think the cops were a bit skeptical, since there were no signs of a break-in. I think they suspect a disgruntled boyfriend."

"Nathaniel Bishop."

"Give it up, Helen. He's never had keys. Nor has anyone but you."

"Hmm."

Annie was glad when Helen sank into a thoughtful silence. She was tired of defending Nate to her best friend. He was always there for her, every time she needed him. He charmed her and excited her and seduced her and protected her.

And she loved him.

Even thinking it made her nervous, but Annie could deny it no longer. She loved Nate Bishop. Admitting it to herself was thrilling…and scary. Now what was she going to do with the information? For the moment, she chose to tuck it away until she was more comfortable sharing, but the thought sat at the back of her mind as Helen parked and they went to their separate businesses.

Upon entering her office, Annie got another unpleasant piece of news—a message from Gloria, who was sick with some stomach bug. Great. She would be working alone all day. Then again, at least she wouldn't have to be giving any further explanations for a while.

But that one ray of sunshine dissipated the moment she saw Clive Hardy outside the shop. He was admiring the new window, which she'd just unveiled.

Not looking forward to being alone with him, she steeled herself when he swung open the shop door and stepped inside.

"I was very angry with you, Annie," Hardy began as he stalked toward her. "I couldn't understand why you wouldn't let me in before…but now I do."

"You do?"

"Yes, of course. You wanted to surprise me." He glanced back at the display window. "You were thinking of me when you created your new masterpiece."

Annie frowned. "What in the world gave you that idea?"

"You know me so very well." He turned back to her and practically ate her up with his intense gaze. "I might be mild mannered on the outside, but as only *you* know, underneath my business suits, I'm really Superdick."

Annie choked. "Excuse me?" Part of her wanted to laugh, but this guy really creeped her out.

"I know you want me, Annie, and now you can have me," Hardy said, his tone wheedling. "With that harridan who works for you gone, we have the whole shop to ourselves." He reached out as if to touch her.

Leaping back, she slapped at his grabbing hand. "Get out." She was so angry, her pulse was thundering through her ears.

His features puckered. "No more games, Annie, not between us."

"I'm not playing a game. That's an order. Get out and stay out! I don't need your business bad enough to put up with you anymore."

"You can't kick me out of here!" he protested.

"Either go on your own or I'll call the police and they can escort you out. And I'll get a court order to make sure you stay away from me, too. The police are going to want to talk to you, anyway," Annie informed him, just in case they hadn't gotten to him yet. "I've told them all about you, you—you pervert."

With a furious glare, Hardy backed away from her

toward the front door, muttering, "I'll make you pay for that, bitch!"

Annie's pulse jagged even harder at the whispered threat. Her attacker had whispered, had called her a bitch, as well. Clive Hardy? Could it be?

He slammed out of the shop, and Annie's mind whirled with the possibility.

She hadn't exactly gotten a look at her attacker. Or been able to tell how big he was. He'd been strong, though.

Just as Hardy so obviously thought he was. *Super-dick?* She shuddered.

"Good riddance to bad rubbish!"

She was sure the cops would have a good laugh at this story when she filled them in later. Something nagged at her about the encounter though, something she couldn't quite put together.

On the alert for a return performance, Annie never quite settled down all day. Not that she was jumping at shadows—she simply had this overwhelming sense of unease that wouldn't let her alone.

The phone ringing had her jumping out of her skin. She grabbed up the receiver, expecting to hear some new whispered threat. So it was quite a relief to hear a familiar voice saying, "Hi, beautiful. How's your morning so far?"

"Nate!" Thank heavens. "Gloria is out sick and I had a visit from the customer from hell, Clive Hardy. I'm beginning to think he might have been my mid-night visitor."

"What did he do?"

"He came on to me, but don't worry," she added

quickly. "Nothing happened. I sent him packing and told him never to darken my doorstep again."

"Have you notified the authorities?"

"I will," she promised.

"Good. I got hold of my security guy. He can come take a look at your place this afternoon to see what he can do for you."

"I can't get away."

"I can make the time."

Thankfully, she'd given him a set of keys that morning so that he could see to Rock while she was at Helen's. "What would I do without you?" she asked.

"I hope I'll never have to know."

Hanging up, she was in a better mood, if hungry again. And customers were streaming into the shop. Because Gloria was out, Annie couldn't leave the store for lunch, so she called Helen for a rescue. Awhile later, her friend brought her a sandwich, a brownie, iced coffee and the news that Nick had done one of his disappearing acts again.

"How can you be sure with Nick?" Annie asked, then took a bite of the sandwich.

For the moment, she was between customers. Only a pair of young women were browsing.

"I checked for your keys and they're gone."

"You checked everywhere?"

"I keep them in one place—my top drawer in back. And they're not anywhere to be found, and neither is Nick. I wanted to talk to him about the keys—I thought maybe he had them for some reason. Now who knows when we'll be able to ask him?"

"He may be back later. He could be on a shoot."

"His backpack is gone."

Annie asked, "And you know this how?"

"I checked his place. I have *his* keys, too, you know."

"Nick had no reason to go to my place," Annie said thoughtfully. "Who else knew the keys were there?"

Helen shrugged. "*I* never told anyone but Nick."

Maybe the spare keys being gone at the same time someone had gotten into her place without a sign of a break-in was just a coincidence, but Annie thought not. And from Helen's expression, Annie guessed they were on the same wavelength. More information for the authorities.

Her chance came soon after Helen left and Annie had taken care of a customer who came in for a pair of panties, claiming she had somehow lost hers. *Right.*

Detective John Sanchez called her from the district office and identified himself as being in charge of her case. She told him about Clive Hardy and about the missing spare keys. But when he asked if she thought Hardy would have known about the keys, much less had the opportunity to get at them, she had to answer honestly. No.

Detective Sanchez asked her to call him if anything else happened, and said that he would keep her informed from his end.

Throughout the afternoon, thoughts of her stalker plagued her whenever she wasn't busy with a customer. Why couldn't she put it together? This was happening to *her,* so she was the best person to figure it out, right?

The spare keys seemed to be central to figuring out the identity of her stalker, considering there had been no sign of forcible entry to her place.

Who, other than Helen and Nick, had access? Helen's employees, she guessed, but they were mostly college kids and didn't even know her.

Wondering if security guards normally had keys to everything, Annie guessed she should ask Nate about it. She hadn't ruled out Harry Burdock, after all. If he had free access to all the businesses, he could have gotten into Helen's Cybercafé and found Annie's keys. Her initials had been on the ring so that Helen could easily identify them. Maybe he had, too. That would explain how those photographs of her in her home had gotten into her personal mail, she thought, remembering the big man she'd suspected was the security guard.

The last customer had gone and Annie had locked the front door before she remembered she hadn't opened the day's mail. Wondering if she should leave it until the next day, she thought about going to Helen's place alone and decided against it. She'd wait until her friend was ready to leave for the night, which gave her plenty of catch-up time.

It wasn't until she'd gotten to the bottom of the stack that she found the plain manilla envelope sans stamps or address.

Now what?

Pulse hammering, she held the envelope in her hands for a moment before opening it. A peek inside revealed more photographs. Annie closed her eyes, fearing to look as she slid them out of the envelope across her desk.

Then she faced her worst nightmare.

Stunned, she could hardly breathe as she spread the photographs out like a hand of cards. But rather than kings or queens, the images on the deck were of her and Nate, tracing their progress as they'd made love in the display window.

The display...*Superdick*...that was it!

She searched the window area for a camera—one of those spy tools the cops had talked about—but found nothing. Then, looking at the photos again, she realized the angle wasn't head-on. They'd been taken from above, thereby avoiding the fabric for the most part—probably snapped from the second floor of the building across the street.

Annie stuffed the evidence back into the envelope, headed out the shop's rear door and made for the stairs.

Nate needed to know about these. He needed to know that Clive Hardy had been aware of the Superman costume beneath the mannequin's suit. And Hardy *couldn't* have known if he hadn't been keeping watch on her somehow while she'd worked on the window. That's what had bothered her about his visit.

By the time she got to the third floor, she was breathless and yet energized. And so walking into Nate's office and not finding anyone there was disheartening. He had to be around, she thought. He would never leave the place unlocked.

"Nate?" she called, before entering his private office.

Empty.

"Damn! Nate, where the heck are you?"

She needed to share this latest evidence, and the

man she loved was the only one to whom she would dare show these pictures. *Unless the police insisted,* she amended, not liking that thought one bit. It might have been dark in that display window, but the camera work had been professional. Both she and Nate could be identified...not to mention their various body parts.

Never having seen the inner office before, Annie thought how much it reminded her of Nathaniel. Of a lawyer's office. Dark woods and neutrals. No bright colors. No artwork. Nothing to set it off. No trace of the man she'd fallen for.

She couldn't deny it any longer: she really was in love. And she had a dilemma that she needed to solve, and soon. She needed to believe in Nathaniel as well as in Nate. They were, as he had reminded her more than once, the same man. She couldn't help the panic in her chest every time she tried to merge them in her mind.

"Come on, Nate, where are you?" she muttered as she circled the room and came to a stop at his desk.

She stared at his work area, so neat compared to hers. But then, this was Nathaniel's desk, she reminded herself, not really Nate's.

Not knowing where he was or when he would be back was so frustrating. Annie was too anxious to stand around and wait. Maybe she ought to leave him a note and then go find Helen. But of course, there were no pens or notepads marring his perfect desk.

Annie went around to the other side and pulled open the center drawer, where she found a pen. A look-see in the top, righthand drawer produced a pad of paper, which she pulled out. About to close the drawer, she hesitated when a piece of ecru stationery caught her eye.

She sank down in his chair and stared. And when her heart settled, she reached in and pulled out a sheet with lacy texture across the top. *The same stationery used by her admirer!*

"Annie, there you are."

Dressed in his leathers, Nate stood in the doorway, his gaze pinned to the delicate piece of paper in her hand.

Her mouth went dry and she acknowledged how much she wanted him, even having found this...this proof of his perfidy. The single sheet slipped from her fingers, but she gathered herself together to open the envelope and spread the photographs over his desk.

Aware that he was stalking across the room toward her, she said, "Nice work," though her voice was as stiff as her shoulders.

She watched him carefully as he glanced down at the photographs. His features froze into a mask and he met her gaze.

"Where did these come from?"

"You tell me."

He shook his head as if he couldn't believe what he was hearing. "You think I had something to do with this?"

"Not at first, no," she said softly, when what she really wanted to do was yell. What she really wanted to do was demand an explanation. Ask him how he could make her fall in love with him and then betray her like this. "Not until I found the stationery."

"I can explain."

"I'm sure you can." He wasn't doing a very good

job of hiding his guilt, she thought, watching his face. "And you *will.* To the police."

That made him start and demand, "Why are you doing this?"

"Me? *I'm* doing something I shouldn't?"

"Yes."

"And that would be?"

"Believing I'm your stalker. That I would terrify you and try to hurt you."

"Oh, come on, Nate, admit it. What exactly have you been doing? Playing with my head so that I would turn to you and you could use creative sex to console me?"

It made sense, considering she never had been physically hurt.

Annie went over everything that had happened to her and realized that, as owner of the building, Nate had access to the café and to her keys. Why hadn't she thought of that? He'd been around at just the right moment so often—because he had been the one stalking and photographing her. Only it was worse, because he must have had someone else photograph her.

"Where did *that* conclusion come from?" he asked.

Furious with herself for being so blind, for putting her emotions on the line, she said, "You're always talking about danger—"

"That's Nate, not me."

"What?"

"You see us as different men, right? Oh, no, wait...Nate's not actually a man. I forgot. He's a fantasy, so he's entitled to be or do whatever he wants."

"So you're admitting you did this."

Nate sighed. "No, Annie, I'm asking you to start seeing who I really am."

"I see, all right."

She tried to walk past him to the door, but he caught her upper arm and swung her around to face him. The breath caught in her throat and pressure built in her chest as she looked into his eyes.

"No," he said, "you really don't see, or you would know that I played into your fantasies because I finally understood that's what you wanted, what you demanded. You wouldn't give me—Nathaniel—a break. I didn't know what to do. And then I took a really good look at your displays and realized a direct approach was never going to work with you, that you would expect something more subtle and more exotic."

"You figured that out from my windows?"

"And from talking with Nick."

"Nick?" Shocked, Annie tried to fathom her friend's betrayal. "He was in on this?"

"He wasn't in on anything. I just asked him for some advice at the beginning because he knew you better than almost anyone." Nate shrugged. "Then for some reason, he changed his mind and suggested that I stay away from you."

After she'd asked Nick to investigate him, Annie thought, remembering what he'd learned. "Who holds the mortgage to your building?"

"What?"

"Is it Frank Mancuso?"

"Mancuso? Who has been filling your head with such nonsense? Helen?"

"You know, it doesn't matter." Especially since she needed to end this. "Forget I asked."

"My father," Nate said. "As much as he thought I was making a mistake, he gave me a personal loan, so that I could follow my own dream. It's the reason I still do work for him occasionally."

Could she believe him? And if it were true, where had Nick gotten his misinformation? Annie remembered he hadn't been willing to tell her the source.

"Annie, am I getting through to you at all?" Nate asked, grasping her shoulders as if desperate.

His mere touch sent desire coursing through her. Annie took a big breath and steadied herself. Nate might be her stalker, but he still had power over her. Realizing that made her start to panic again.

"Let me go, Nate. You and I are through."

"Don't say that!" His expression tight and angry, he nevertheless did as she asked. But he didn't back off. "I want all of you, Annie, and you have to want all of me if this is going to work between us. Fantasy isn't enough for me, and it shouldn't be for you."

Her whole world had just been turned upside down and he seemed to be talking about love? Another ploy, perhaps?

"Stop trying to confuse me."

"I'm trying to make you understand that I love you, Annie Wilder, and that you don't have to protect yourself from *me.* Yes, I wrote those letters, but the only thing I'm guilty of was being crazy enough to do whatever it took to get you to notice me and fall for me. I figured you would catch on once we really connected." He sounded truly disappointed that she hadn't.

Annie fixated on one fact. "So you're admitting you wrote the letters."

"Yeah, I wrote them. But as for those photographs or stalking you, you're dead wrong. I love you, Annie," he said for a third time. "Trust me. Let me see you through this."

"I—I can't."

He shook his head. "You don't want to. You want your stalker to be me because then you can stay safe. You can tell yourself you were right to keep a piece of yourself back, a piece I couldn't get to. Then you don't have to put your heart on the line and see where it leads you. You can tell yourself I'm just another Alan Cooper and wash your hands of me."

Unable to take any more, Annie ran out of the office and away from the one man who had the power to destroy her. How could she have let it get this far?

She had to talk to Helen. To tell her friend everything. Helen would probably be delighted. Would say "I told you so!"

No, that wasn't fair. Helen loved her and wanted the best for her.

What if Nate was telling the truth? Could he be innocent? Could he be right that she *wanted* him to be guilty so that she wouldn't have to face her feelings for him? So that she wouldn't have to make a commitment?

Not liking that thought at all, Annie flew into the café, heart pounding, but stopped short when she didn't see the blonde. "Is Helen in back?"

"Sorry, she's not here," the kid behind the counter said. He was cleaning up, getting ready to close the place.

"I need to find her right away."

"Riley was in here awhile ago, looking for her, too. Maybe she's across the street with him."

"Thanks."

Annie headed for Gallery R and prayed Helen was there. They could leave and get some dinner and a couple of strong drinks. Then when they got home, they could rant and cry together.

After that, Annie could call Detective John Sanchez, fill him in on the new photographs and Nate's being her admirer and very probably her stalker.

And then she could go back to her safe solitude and the furry male in her life....

15

NATE DIDN'T KNOW how long he sat there after Annie left. He thought he could leave it up to her, and if she didn't believe him, tough. The police couldn't prove he was involved in anything, any more than she could.

But then he started thinking about it. He couldn't blame her for being scared or suspicious of him, could he? So many scary things had happened to her, and he was always around afterward.

And the truth of it was, he still wanted her. He still loved her. So he got off his duff and locked up and went downstairs in search of the woman who'd been his obsession longer than he cared to admit.

Annie's Attic was locked up tight, alarm on, as he figured it would be, so he entered Helen's Cybercafé in hopes of finding her there. No Annie.

No Nick, either. But when he turned around, it was to see Helen walking in the door.

"I'm back."

"Hey, Annie was looking for you," the kid behind the counter said.

"So what did she do? Leave?" Helen locked gazes with Nate. "Go back to my place?"

''She said something about checking over at the gallery to see if you were there.''

''The gallery? I'd better get over there.''

''Hold up.'' Nate got between her and the door. ''I think you and I need to talk.''

Helen looked him over. ''You're right. I figured out who took Annie's keys from my drawer, which means I probably know the identity of her stalker.''

A pulse ticked at the corner of Nate's eye as he waited for her to accuse him.

HELEN WASN'T IN GALLERY R and Annie was waiting, growing more impatient by the minute, while Riley took care of a customer. He glanced at her sideways and gave her the high sign that he'd be with her in a few minutes. Though Annie understood the importance of hanging on to a potential sale, especially a big one, if the size of the canvas were any indication, she couldn't help but be impatient. Like a child, she thought. She wanted Helen and she wanted her now.

Was that the way she'd been with Nate? The familiarity of the mental demand spoke volumes. And maybe she was ready to listen.

Wandering around the gallery, only half seeing the pieces of art, she wondered if Nate had been right about her. If she would rather think he was guilty so that she wouldn't have to put her heart at risk. The more she thought about it, the more uneasy she grew.

Nate wasn't the stalker type. He was up front with his dangerous seductions. He'd done only as much as she'd allowed, and had stopped whenever she'd wanted to call a halt. He'd engaged her, enticed her, seduced her. And she simply didn't believe he would hurt her, physically or mentally. Now that she'd had time to cool off, she regretted her accusations.

What was she going to do?

Annie shook her head and tried to distract herself by concentrating on the artwork before her. She happened to be standing by that display of photographs of nearly nude women, the one she'd given Nate a hard time over the other night.

About to walk away, she realized there was something familiar about the photographs. The women weren't posing for the camera. They were unaware of its presence…just as she had been!

Other similarities struck her as well, and she looked for the artist's signature. There were only initials: J.R.

The pulse in her throat snapped and she moved to the end of the display, where she found a monograph about sexuality written by the artist. Gaping, she whirled around to leave and came face-to-face with a smiling John Riley.

"I finally got rid of that bozo. He wasn't interested in buying anything. What a waste of time."

"It was you," she gasped, feeling a little lightheaded at the realization. "It was you all along."

Riley glanced at his exhibit and then at her. "So you recognize my style."

He smiled at her as if she should be pleased. She tried to move past him but he blocked her way.

"No reason to hurry out of here, Annie. Not when I finally have you all to myself."

Pulse spiking, she yelled, "Get out of my way!"

But Riley ignored her, and though she tried to dodge around him, effectively blocked her escape. "All those weeks with me hanging around the café, just waiting to get close to you."

"What about Helen?" she demanded, telling herself to think. She had to get out of here.

"What about her?" he said drolly.

Had she imagined the romance between her friend and the gallery owner? Annie wondered. Had she just been seeing what she wanted to see?

"Charming," she muttered, "but I really have to go."

"I don't think so." Riley managed to stay between her and the door, and locked it before she could get her hand on the knob. Then he snapped off a bank of lights, throwing the gallery into semidarkness, with little more light than she'd had while working on the display. Reminded of being trapped first in the janitor's closet and then in her own home, Annie found her heart beginning to thud. This time the monster was with her.

"I don't get it," she said, her mind racing, trying to think of a way out. At the same time she couldn't help wondering why he would go to the lengths he had to get her attention.

"Neither do I. What's with you and Bishop?" Riley asked, sounding like a jealous lover. "What in the hell are you doing with an uptight businessman rather than a kindred spirit like me?"

"You're no kindred spirit."

"We have so much in common, Annie." He was stalking her and she was backing up across the room as he continued. "It's time you realized that. When I heard about the letters from your admirer, that they turned you on, I knew how alike we were. And I knew just what you wanted."

"The photos?" Swallowing hard, Annie shook her head. "The letters were romantic and tantalizing. The photos were simply crude. What do you think you've been doing, invading my privacy, terrorizing me—"

"Why, I've been making love to you the way you like it."

"That's sick!"

Riley's expression darkened. "What do you call screwing Bishop in the store window?"

That was it! Annie made her move. She flew toward the door, but before she could release the lock, Riley was on her. Arm around her waist, he pulled her toward the back of the gallery, at the same time trying to get a hand under her skirt. Annie screamed and elbowed him.

"Let go of me, you sick bastard!"

"I'm not letting you go now that I finally have you where I want you."

Riley spoke in a voice that made the hairs on her neck stand at attention. She recognized that whisper from the phone calls. One of his hands was groping her, sliding up her stomach to her breast. She thought she might be sick...and decided she should do so on him.

"I'm disappointed that you aren't more in tune with me, of course," he was saying. "Not that it matters. I intend to get what you've freely given Bishop."

A sharp bang whipped her attention to the front

door. As if summoned, Nate was there, trying to get in, and a crazed-looking Helen was right beside him.

"Screw them!" Riley growled, dragging her back behind the exhibit.

Annie fought him for all she was worth, kicking and clawing, but her backward blows were ineffectual.

"No!" she yelled, frantically grabbing on to a heavy piece of sculpture and jerking them to a stop.

Still he didn't loosen his grip. "Annie, don't make me hurt you."

Riley was pressed into her back, trying to lift her skirt again and grinding his hips into her butt, letting her know the struggle was turning him on. If she could get her hand on that part of him...

"They won't get in here," he whispered in her ear. "And if they go for help, it will be too late, because by then you'll be mine."

Annie reached back to grab him, but he was ready for her and caught her hand in a vise. He began to squeeze....

And then she heard it: an angry buzz drawing closer.

"What the hell?"

Riley loosened his grip for a second and Annie used the opportunity to grab the sculpture, wrest it from its base and push it at him. Then she ran for the door. But when she realized what Nate was about, she veered off toward the left side of the gallery and sheltered her head and face.

For a moment, she saw the plate glass blaze brilliantly with light—until the Harley jumped upward and shattered it. Nate came roaring into the gallery in a spray of glass chips.

Riley yelled something. And Annie saw him holding his eyes—no doubt cut by flying glass. Appropriate in a sick way, she thought.

Before Nate could get off the Harley, Annie rushed forward and threw herself on him, covering him with grateful kisses.

"You're better than any fantasy," she told him apologetically.

The lights went on. Helen had come through the broken glass. Now she headed for the back saying, "Don't let that bastard get away. I'm calling the police."

RILEY HAD BEEN TAKEN away after admitting to everything but defacing Annie's Attic and trying to ruin her business—he'd suggested the police look to the alderman's cohorts. For all the good that would do, Annie thought wryly, though she was certain he was correct. No doubt Zavadinski hadn't dirtied his own hands.

"You were right, you know," she told Nate.

"About?"

They were in the café, just the three of them, the place being closed for the night. But Helen had offered some herbal tea and Annie had thought it a splendid idea. Anything to keep Nate from going away before she could apologize.

"My fear of being with you," she said. "The reason I let myself be convinced that you were my stalker."

"I helped on that score," Helen admitted. "Sorry. Really. I'm just a little overprotective of my friends."

"Which isn't really a bad thing," Nate said.

Helen patted his shoulder. "I'll leave now. I'll be over there if you need me."

Helen slunk back behind the counter and redid work that had already been done. And Annie took her first truly easy breath in days.

"I just wish you could have listened to me earlier," Nate was saying as the front door opened.

Expecting to see Nick back from wherever he'd disappeared to, Annie was surprised when a woman entered, and was even more surprised that, after everything that had happened, Helen had forgotten to lock the door. She looked as if she meant to turn the prospective customer away. A bit too classy for the neighborhood, the woman was expensively dressed, and her silver-blond hair was smoothed back from her face in an elegant French twist.

"I did listen," Annie said, turning her attention back to Nate. "I just ran scared. But when I stopped to take a breath, I thought about what you said. And I realized you were right. I knew in my heart of hearts that you weren't a stalker. But I waited about a minute too long to come to that conclusion."

"And put yourself right in Riley's grasp."

"Exactly." She shuddered and glanced toward the two women. The stranger was forcing her card on Helen, who shrugged and took it from her. "I know you probably can't forgive me," Annie continued, "but I wanted you to know—"

"What exactly are you saying?"

Annie gulped and said, "I'm trying to apologize."

"Are you saying you're willing to do things differently?"

"Do things differently," she echoed, surprised that he wanted to do anything with her at all after she'd been so horrid to him. "What does that mean? No more fantasies?"

"I have a great fantasy I'd like to explore."

"As in?"

"Keeping a closer eye on you on a far more regular basis."

"As in..." Could she say the words? She could. "Live together?"

Nate looked at her long and hard, then grinned. "That'll do for a start."

Annie grinned back, and when Nate kissed her, her imagination began to soar....

"Ahem."

Annie broke the kiss and glared up at Helen, who said, "I hate to interrupt, but did you see that woman?"

"We saw her," Nate said. "And you love interrupting."

Helen's cheeks filled with color. "I'll let that go for tonight, but after that..." She turned to Annie. "The woman was looking for Nick. She said it was urgent, and she gave me this."

Annie took a look at the card—not a business card, but a calling card, beautifully designed and executed. "Isabel Grayson. Sounds familiar."

"If I'm not mistaken, she's the daughter of Senator William Grayson," Helen stated.

"You would be correct," Nate said.

Annie frowned. "What would she want with Nick?"

"That's what I was wondering."

"Frankly, I don't care," Nate suddenly announced. He rose, pulling Annie with him. "Nick's a big boy. He can take care of himself. Isabel Grayson, too, I'm sure."

"But—"

"Say good-night, Annie."

"Good night," she repeated dutifully, before Nate dragged her outside and over to his Harley.

"Now where were we?" he asked, pressing her back into the bike.

"Uh-uh. Not here."

"What not here?" he teased.

"I know the wheels in that perverted mind of yours are turning. I have a perfectly good bed, which I've been dying to try. And a cat who probably thinks I've abandoned him."

"We have to use the bed?" he complained as he straddled the bike. "Well, if we have to...get on."

Annie hesitated. "Um, you do realize I'm wearing a skirt."

Nate raised his eyebrows. "And that would be a problem why?"

"Crotchless panties," she lied, just to tease him.

"You *would* go and plant that picture in my mind," he groused.

And it put a picture in her own mind, too....

On the Harley, Nate unzipped his leathers and released his full erection. She threw a leg over the bike in front of him, then licked her fingers to part the lips between her legs, and used them to give him the most intimate of kisses. With a breathy sigh, she slid down his length and settled against him, looking forward to the ride of her life....

Annie climbed on behind Nate and wrapped her arms around his waist.

"Bed, huh?"

"If you're good," she murmured in his ear, "I'll let you..."

Then, just the way he liked her to, she told him in graphic terms exactly what she wanted.

* * * * *

The CHICAGO HEAT miniseries by

Patricia Rosemoor

continues in September 2002!

Look for Nick's exciting story in #55

IMPROPER CONDUCT.

Enjoy!